Haunted By The Succubus

MICHELLE DOREY

The Haunted Ones 3
Paranormal Suspense

ISBN: 978-1-988913-11-7
Monarch Moments
Cover Design by Juan Padron
https://www.instagram.com/padrondesign/
Edited by Paula Grundy
https://paulaproofreader.wixsite.com/home

100719PRT

CONTENTS

ONE

I've always known things. Stuff that people try to hide under a plastic smile as they go about their day-to-day lives, bang around in my head all the time. It can get pretty distracting when you're in a crowd, but thankfully, I learned how to handle it at a very young age. Otherwise, I'd probably be in an insane asylum. Nope, all I do now is relegate the noise to a junk pile in the back of my head.

But sometimes I slip up and get steamrolled.

Take that girl up ahead, waiting at the bus stop. No wait. Let me. She's gorgeous. The ragged designer jeans hugging model-thin thighs, the blond, tousled mane framing a face that flaunts indifference; the total effect carefully crafted and expensive. But it can't erase the fact that she's shrouded in a muddy green haze. I don't even give her a second look as I pass by.

That girl has more issues than a 7-Eleven magazine rack. The worry that her boyfriend is cheating on her causes a crease in her perfectly applied makeup. I could tell her that the constant self-deprecating mantra playing in her head, is anything but true. But why bother? She'd think I was some kind of freak.

Which I am.

Besides, at twenty-five, she's too old for me. I'm barely nineteen and a high school dropout to boot. She'd give me the same look as if she stepped on a wad of chewed bubblegum.

I wait for the light to turn green and then hustle across the intersection. Late again for a job that barely covers my rent, let alone food. But even so, it beats living with my parents and the shining star who is my older brother Seth. I miss my little sister, though. Amy was the peacekeeper, the only one of my family who actually "got" me.

When I open the door to the courier shop, Hilda looks over and waves before continuing her conversation on the phone. There are two order slips waiting on the counter. The first pickup is at a florist which will take me to the outskirts of town for the delivery. I'm reading the second when a hard shove on my back makes my head snap back.

Even before I wheel around, I know it's Phil.

"You're late! Two more minutes, and I was gonna have to do these." He stands with arms resembling gnarled tree trunks folded across his chest. The usual sneer is plastered to his lips and small piggy eyes.

"Bite me, loser." I turn away reading the second order. It's a weak comeback, but the guy could break me like a twig. He spends every free minute at the gym pumping iron and downing protein shakes. He's a full head taller than me and outweighs me by at least fifty pounds. Of muscle. Damn.

Hilda hangs the phone up with a resounding bang. "Philip! Sometimes, I swear if you weren't my sister's kid, I'd toss your sorry ass out of here." She shoots a hard look at me. "Adam, you *are* late again. Consider this your last warning. One more and..." Her voice trails off, and she takes the keys that Phil hands her.

"Sorry. I got caught up in the game again. It won't happen anymore. I promise." I turn my head a bit, so I'm looking at her from the corner of my eyes. I call it 'sidey-eyes', and when I do it I'm able to see Hilda's aura. She's that clear green like a newly mowed lawn, just like normal. Not a trace of the red that flares when she's really mad, so I know she's bluffing. Truth be told, she likes me more than Philip, and who could blame her? He's a bully and not overly bright. I can do five orders in one run, planning a route that doesn't waste a drop of gas in the process.

Yeah, I know. That's not exactly Mensa material.

She finishes writing out the order from the phone call and hands it to me. Phil takes that opportunity to grunt a "see ya later" and slip out the front door.

"You know, if you applied yourself a little more and took on more hours, you could be an assistant manager. I'm not going to work here forever, get carried feet first out of the store like what happened to my dad." She leans on the counter and flashes a smile at me. It isn't the first time she's asked me to assume more responsibility. She's in her late fifties—hell, she's going to turn sixty real soon. And… she's *tired.* Not sick with some kind of cancer or disease. I'd know that. Just worn out like an old boot that's seen too many winters. The woman's worked hard since she was a young girl, and is running out of gas.

She bats her eyes. "So, what do you say? Pitch in more here, and the assistant manager slot's yours for the asking, Adam."

I snort. "Ya, that'd go over well with Phil all right. He'd probably break every bone in my body. You trying to get me killed or something?"

She pushes up from the counter and sighs. "My father would roll over in his grave if I let Phil run the place. The only muscle that boy needs to exercise is between his ears, but I think it's already atrophied beyond use."

I sidey-eye a look over her shoulder. Yep. Her father nods his wispy gray head in agreement and casts a smile at his daughter.

That's another thing that I can do. I see ghosts.

Certain places and people are magnets attracting spiritual essence. Hilda and this place keep her dad around. I wish it were that simple where I'm concerned but like everything else about me, it's complicated. I'd give anything to see and chat with my grandmother's spirit but she never comes. Instead, spirits I barely care about or who I don't even know are drawn to me.

"I'm sure your father would be proud of what you've done here, Hilda. You buried the competition and tripled the amount of business." A glance past her shoulder takes in the old guy's nod while his rail-thin chest puffs out like a banty rooster.

"See? That's what I mean." She points her chin at me. "Look, Adam, you've worked here for what—six months? Yet you have a really good handle on what's going on, here! You easily assessed the growth—"

I cut her off. "Which would be even more if you set up a better website and did some stuff with Google search ads!"

She laughed. "See? You get the lay of the land, and what can be over the horizon while Phil does well to tie his shoes." She shakes her head and waves of exasperation slide from her shoulders.

"I'll think about it." I pluck the order slip and keys from her and head to the back door where the van is parked. I hate leading her on, and what's worse is that she knows I'm fudging. I pause for a moment. "Want me to pick up some lunch for you when I'm out?"

She reaches under the counter and holds up a brown bag with her lunch. "Thanks, but I'm opting for healthy."

I nod, pushing the door to go out into the back lot. The day is warm even for May, with the sun casting a glint on the windshield. As I wander around the vehicle inspecting it for any damage that Phil may have done, which of course he'd blame on me, I wonder how my sister is doing. It's been six months since I've seen Amy. Email and Skype aren't the same as actually hanging out together, watching a movie or something.

And the fact that I'd left just before Christmas and missed seeing her face when she opened my gift still leaves me with a hollow feeling.

I get in the van and start the engine, trying to shake off the remorse. The blowup with my parents that day had been a storm hulking on the horizon for like forever. It was a hurricane of a fight, but the worst part was Amy's tears streaming down her face before I closed the door. That image haunts me.

TWO

The problem with doing this job is that it takes so little mental effort. As I drive first to the florist and then to the automotive shop to pick up the packages, that last scene with my parents spools on a loop in my head.

I'd skipped school again. But unlike the times before, my parents received an email from the guidance counselor. Just my luck that the teachers had nothing better to do on their lunch break but talk about Adam Rafferty pissing away 'real academic potential'. What made it more stark was the contrast with 'Wonder Boy', my older brother Seth.

That day, Mom had even left work early to come home to have it out with me. It didn't help that she's a teacher herself, albeit for grade six. She'd lit into me like a banshee, screaming so hard that the vein in her temple stuck out. But Dad pushed it over the top when he came home, grounding me and trying to take away my phone, my gaming shit, and any use of the car, EVER! Snippets of the lecture, I could recite by heart since it still rings in my ears. 'Underachiever' was the best of it, although 'lazy bum' and 'loser' came a close second and third.

What they didn't understand was how irrelevant school had

become for me. Why pretend to give a shit about quadratic equations or expository compositions? And if atoms and molecules are the basic building blocks of everything, how come I can see spirits and the energy field of every living thing?

And at the end of the day, does working your ass off, getting deeper in debt to get the vaunted sheepskin from a college make you any happier? How come success isn't measured in terms of happiness instead of money?

But explaining this to two people who had to work three jobs in order to get an education and get ahead would be like trying to explain to a dog why it should want to become a cat.

At the blaring honk behind me, I glance up at the traffic light which is now green. If it weren't for the van's Rabbit Express logo emblazoned on the side panels I'd flip the bird at that asshat laying on his horn. Seriously? Two seconds of the guy's life, and he has to make it a thing.

I pull into an empty parking spot in front of the dry cleaner's and get out. With any luck the cute girl working there the last time I was in is there today. She's not drop-dead gorgeous, but I can tell she's a good person, not stuck on herself. She's kind of shy like Rebecca had been.

Rebecca. My first love before her family got posted to Pensacola. At first we Skyped and texted every day. Then there were gaps of a day, becoming a week, then weeks, before she wrote me that she'd found someone new.

An old-fashioned bell clangs against the door as I enter. My heart flips into my stomach when I see the girl look up from behind the counter. She's got these deep pools of ebony eyes that I could fall into forever. And the pink haze surrounding her clinches it for me. I'm a sucker for girls with that glow. They're like cotton candy on the outside but steel inside when it comes to loyalty. Too bad Rebecca's hadn't been pink. She might have waited for me.

But this girl's got it in spades. With a smile as bright as the sun outside, she says, "Hi. You here for the Johnson pickup?" Even her voice is soft and sweet. Her cheeks have a fresh glow. No need for layers of makeup. Am I crushing on her? Duh!

"Yeah." The word comes out as a croak, and I clear my throat, noting her amused smile before she turns. I let myself probe a little, trying to keep my hopes at a manageable level. No boyfriend. Bonus! But there's something worrying her. I can see darker threads in her aura. Her mother. She just found out her mother has breast cancer. Shit.

She hands me the clothes all pressed and packaged in the cellophane. "They already paid for the cleaning."

"Great." I take the bundle and hesitate, looking at her. "You're new here, aren't you? I'm Adam from Rabbit Express." I extend my hand hopefully.

When she takes it, murmuring, "I'm Polly," another image jolts from the touch of her hand right into my head. It's the face of a red-haired girl, eyes closing as she draws closer, the slightly parted lips, saturated with love and desire as she's about to be kissed.

Great. Polly's gay and has a girlfriend. Just my luck.

"Well. Nice to meet you. I guess I'll be seeing you sometimes. This store is one of our accounts." I take my hand back and then head for the door. She's not for me, but still... she's nice. I turn and look at her. "They do amazing things with breast cancer patients. I saw a documentary on it last week. Your mom's going to pull through the surgery. See ya!"

I turn again before she has a chance to say anything and before I can see that look of shock in her eyes. I've seen it too many times before on people's faces when I tell them their private thoughts.

I know I stepped over the line in telling her that. Nana would never have approved. She saw my gifts, the psychic talent I was born with at a really young age. She had it too. She always wanted to shelter me and warned me against saying too much to people. But as usual, I don't always follow advice. Even from someone as wise as Nana had been.

She was right about keeping it from Mom and Dad. They would have had me tested for autism, Asperger's, or some other thing. Amy knows about it, of course. We'd make a game of it, walking down the street with me telling her stuff about strangers going by us. Some of it I made up just to hear her laugh. She had a laugh like small Christmas bells jingling, a bright tinkling of pure joy. Before I start the van I pull my cell phone out to send her a text.

Hey! How r u? I just met the girl of my dreams and she's gay. Good thing Wonder Boy's around to keep the Raffterty gene pool going. Have you started the countdown to summer vacation yet?

I hit send and then slip my phone into my pocket. It buzzes right away, and I look to see her reply. But it's only Hilda with a few new stops scheduled for me. Oh well. Amy's probably still in class anyway.

***

By the time I finish work the sun is a fiery ball on the horizon. After entering the old brick building, I go up the two flights of stairs to my apartment trying not to notice the cooking smells wafting in the air—a mishmash of seared meat, fish and cabbage. As I pass the second floor level, the half-deaf old lady in 2-C yells at some contestant on a TV game show. Thankfully, I don't live in the apartment next to her as the walls are paper thin to begin with.

I share an apartment on the top floor with another guy. Doug is older; he's a twenty-seven-year-old mechanic licking his wounds from a marriage breakup. When his wife called it quits, he needed a roommate to share the rent, and I needed cheap shelter. We don't have all that much in common, so we manage to stay out of each other's way for the most part.

When I enter, Doug is nursing a beer, his feet propped up on the coffee table, watching a movie. He looks over and mumbles a "hi" before turning back to the TV.

"Hey Doug." As I go by him I glance at the TV and see an old John Wayne western, which I know he watched just last week. He's taken creature of habit to a whole other level, which is why he and his wife aren't together anymore. The guy's…well…boring as hell, y'know? It's a great quality for a roomie, but for a life partner?

My cell phone buzzes with a text as soon as I enter my bedroom. I smile seeing Amy's name come up and read what she has to say.

Hi Adam. Heading into the mall with Jess. She says she needs a new pair of jeans but I've got the feeling the dumb-ass jock she's totally hung up on will just happen to be there. No accounting for taste on her part. He's totally stuck on himself!

The next text is a selfie of Amy, cross-eyed and tearing her hair out while her best friend, Jess, is in the background talking to a guy, hanging on his every word. The guy is vaguely familiar.

But it's Amy who makes me smile. Even though she's clowning around contorting her face, it can't hide how cute she is, with the mop of blond curls and big blue eyes.

My thumbs fly sending a reply,

That's Eric Cox's younger brother, isn't it? If he's anything like Eric, yeah...Jess could do better. Sucks to be hanging out there I'm sure. From the look on Jess's face, she probably wouldn't know you were gone if you just left. I would.

Her reply pops up fast.

That's your style not mine, Bro. Are you EVER coming home for a visit? Maybe I'll talk Mom and Dad into letting me take a bus to Watertown. You could show me the sights.

Much as I'd love to see her, it's still too soon. If and when I ever get a place of my own, maybe then. I type a quick reply,

There's not all that much to see to endure the

three hour bus ride getting here. Maybe when you're finished school for the year, I'll come home and we can hang out for a day. Say hi to Jess for me.

An hour later, freshly showered and fed, I leave the apartment on the prowl to my favorite watering hole. It's the only place that didn't card me when I first showed up plus it has the added bonus that a lot of pretty women tend to go there after watching a movie at the theatre next door.

When I enter the joint only a few tables are filled and there are a few empty spots at the gleaming oak bar. The bartender nods and then turns to pour a draft even before I slide onto the stool. I can't decide if this familiar welcome is comforting or a harbinger of a serious drinking problem I'm developing. On the plus side, it helps me sleep, and there's always the long shot that I won't be sleeping alone.

A guy can always hope, right?

I nurse the cold beer glancing at the mirror behind the bar every time the door opening is reflected. And right on time the moviegoers trickle in for a few drinks before they call it a night. And just my good fortune, a couple of girls in their early twenties wander over to sit at the bar beside me.

The one next to me has long chestnut hair and when she settles the faint scent of her perfume drifts from her. She's chatting with her friend who is a petite Asian. Her ruby lipstick is the same shade as her sweater and when she laughs relaying some comic scene in the movie, it reminds me of Amy's laugh.

I turn slightly and smile. "*Game Night.* That's the movie you guys saw, right? It was pretty funny, wasn't it!"

Even though I haven't seen it, I'm picking up snippets from Jane's mind. And her friend Jasmine's as well. I've never met these two girls, but their names flash in my mind, along with the fact that Jane has just finished a two-year relationship, and Jasmine is trying to cheer her up.

Jane grins at me, nodding. "Yeah! What a great movie! You saw it too, right?" She sits back a bit so that Jasmine can take part in the conversation.

"Nope. But I can tell you saw it and loved it."

Her smile fades a bit, and her eyes narrow watching me. "It's pretty popular. And it's the only comedy playing right now." She takes a sip of her rum and coke and then turns to her friend, dismissing me.

But this is what I do, so it's not that easy to shake me off. I lean over the bar smiling at the Asian girl. "Last week you two went to see *Black Panther* and the week before you saw *Jumanji*. You like comedies rather than action movies."

This time it's Jasmine who answers and there's no warmth in her voice, "Yeah. Are you stalking us or something?" She picks up her drink and is about to get up, signaling with a look to her friend, when I quickly add my 'pièce de 'résistance'.

"I read minds, Jasmine." I smile at Jane. "I'm not a stalker, let me assure you. It's just something I do."

Jane puts her hand on Jasmine's arm, stilling her while leaning closer, peering at me. "Oh yeah? What did I have for dinner, if you can read minds?"

I chuckle. "C'mon. Make it something harder than that. I can even smell a bit of garlic on your breath from the shrimp you had."

Jasmine pipes up, "He can't read minds, Jane. He's just saying that. It's a new take on a pickup line. Let's go sit at a table."

But Jane isn't convinced. Either that, or she's not averse to being picked up. Of course that's not mind reading—it's wishful thinking.

"No, wait, Jas. Let me try another question." She sits still, thinking hard, which of course I tune into.

I clear my throat and try my best to look innocent, like this isn't something I do nightly. "Tell you what. Make it the hardest question you can think of. If I'm right, then you go home with me. If I'm wrong, I'll buy you a drink."

Jasmine rolls her eyes and grabs Jane's arm. "Jane! You aren't doing this! You don't even *know* this guy!"

But Jasmine doesn't know what *I do* about Jane. She's kind

of shocked and a little thrilled at my offer. The warm threads of red in her aura give her away, especially that they're emanating from her lower half. It's been a while since she was with her boyfriend, and she's ready for some adventure. The fact I'm also a few years younger makes me safe—"controllable"—in her eyes. Or maybe she knows I'm harmless, no predator, just a horny nineteen-year-old guy. At any rate, she can tell I'm way younger than her.

There's a twinkle in Jane's eye, and her chin raises higher, challenging me with a smile. "Okay. You'll never know this one. What was the name I gave to my first pet?"

Jasmine's not the only one watching this playful exchange. The bartender, Sam, shakes his head smiling as he pours another draft. He knows how this will play out. But there's someone else watching. I can feel a guy's attention, but I'm too taken with Jane, with the soft curve of her smile, as well as the other curves of her totally rocking figure.

"You're sure that's the hardest question you can come up with? Don't get me wrong; I'd give my eye teeth for a date with you, Jane, but I don't want to be accused of taking advantage." I look her in the eye; my smile sly.

"I'm going to enjoy that drink. What's your name, Mr. Mind Reader?" There's a flirty quality to her answer. She's thinking either way it's a win-win for her. I can barely keep myself from giving a fist bump to the universe!

"Adam Rafferty at your service, Miss Jane Elizabeth Montgomery." Yeah, I'm showing off a little.

Her eyes widen, and she slaps my arm playfully, the smile on her face getting wider still.

"You had a gerbil named Fluffy. You wanted a kitten but your mom said no. You had to keep it in your room because your brother Tim is allergic to animal dander. You had Fluffy for almost nine months until you forgot to lock the cage and he escaped, never to be found again. You cried yourself to sleep for three nights after."

"Oh my God! Fluffy! I haven't thought of him in so long. How'd you know?"

"He's right?" Jasmine looks like she's about to have a stroke. "You can't go home with him, Jane."

I'm on a roll now. "You broke up with Eddie Benton two weeks ago. He was a loser who never appreciated you. He was also a lousy lover who *never* satisfied you. I'm not going into why that was, but I know your secret fantasy. It's not sick or twisted like he'd have you think. It's kinky, sure, but sick? Naw."

The smile drips off her face like an ice cream in July, replaced by winter frost in her eyes. Shit! Why didn't I stop at Fluffy? She even pulls back from me a little.

Sam puts the glass of draft in front of me. He's seen me piss away a surefire bet too many times.

Jane rises and slaps a twenty on the bar. "Thanks for making me sound like a total perv in front of all these people. Have a drink and a laugh on *me*, Adam." And with that she and Jasmine huff out of the bar.

Sam shakes his head and drifts down the bar leaving me cursing myself. For all my sensitivity, I never know when to quit while I'm ahead. I could be snuggling up against a hot girl tonight, but thanks to my motor mouth I'm having a cold beer.

Again. The Nineteen-Year-Old Virgin strikes out again. Damn.

I take a long pull on the beer while that older guy takes the stool that Jane vacated.

He cups a glass of whisky that from the look of his raspberry nose he's indulged in too many times to count. There's a faint odor of cigarettes and sweat from a tired sports jacket that's hopeless at trying to contain his paunch belly. "You never give up, do ya kid?"

I look over at him, knowing he's been the guy who I've sensed watching me from time to time. There's no animosity or threat, only a feeling of frustration that I pick up on. And a sort of kindness even though it's the last thing he'd ever admit, even to himself.

"What's it to ya? It's my time to waste, right?" I turn back to my drink, feeling my neck grow warm. It seems Sam isn't the only one to witness me strike out every night.

"You said it, not me. But time's not the only thing you're wasting, kid. You have a gift that you squander for a few drinks. At least do yourself a favor and learn when to shut up. I get more action than you kid, and I'm in my fifties." He made a quick smile. "Must be tough with raging hormones. Think you can lend me some of them? At my age they're not so… abundant." He laughs and downs some more whisky, signaling to Sam for another round.

"Maybe I should take lessons from you, 'Lance Romance'. I can't help rolling my eyes. I may not be Brad Pitt material, but this guy's more like John Goodman than Harrison Ford. And he's bragging about *his* sex life?

He chuckles and extends his hand. "Mike Drogan."

I shake his beefy meat hook, and my mind is flooded with images. A cramped office where the phone rings less and less, a fact that worries him as he barely scraped together last month's rent let alone the one due in a week's time. The only cases he gets in his private investigator business is divorce work which reminds him of his own failed marriage. He retired as a detective from the police department four years ago and promptly lost half his pension when his marriage ended.

"Adam Rafferty. Unfortunate fortune teller at your service."

Mike sits back and sighs, "Now that... that's what I mean about you, kid. You're a self-fulfilling prophesy. I've seen you work. You have a genuine gift, and yet you sabotage yourself even though you target the low-hanging fruit. But what is a real mortal sin is that you're wasting your talent. You could be doing some good with it or even making serious money."

The last thing I need is a lecture from a has-been detective. I heard enough of that sort of crap from my parents, and they had actually accomplished something in life, with good jobs and a nice home and a good marriage. I look over at him and force a smile. "I'm happy with what I do."

"Are you?" His beady, gray eyes skewer me and he holds the probing stare. I may have a gift of reading people but so does he. It's called life. He's seen a lot, and his mind is a steel trap where every kernel of wisdom is snared.

My reply bristles, "Is anyone ever *really* happy? Are you? Forgive me if I'm skeptical of your answer." I turn back to my drink, anxious to end this train wreck of a conversation.

He leans closer. "I know you know all about me. Know that I'm losing business to the slick outfits with the flash but no substance. But at least I'm honest with myself. I try, and sometimes there's a case that gives me a good feeling. Like finding a runaway teen or a lost child. They're the cases I get out of bed every morning for." He's silent for a few beats. "What gets you up each day?"

"My alarm clock." But even though I try to be flip, his words have struck a chord that I don't want to hear.

"Ever think about making more money? I could use someone like you working with me." He takes a sip of his whisky trying to act casual, but this is the real reason he sat next to me. There's some altruism for sure, but he's primarily looking after his own interests.

I turn in my seat and look at him. "Maybe you're right about making more money. But what's stopping me from setting myself up on my own? I don't have to work for you. With my gift, I'd have to turn clients away." I'm teasing, but he doesn't have to know that.

The guffaw that bursts from his throat makes me grin despite myself. "You?" His eyes slide over me. "You're not even of legal drinking age! A teenage private investigator? I've found runaways your age! You wouldn't be taken seriously, kid." He's still smiling when he adds, "Team up with me. I give legitimacy, and you are the seer who will solve the cases."

It's not anything that I ever considered before even though I love police crime drama. And if I could help find a missing kid, save them from predators, it would certainly make me happier than devising the most efficient delivery route. I could try it part time and still keep my job which pays the bills. Mike couldn't pay me... at least not yet.

"So we'd be partners? Fifty fifty?" I watch his face light up for a moment.

"Sixty forty. You get the forty since I've got the name and reputation. We'll see how it works out and talk later about the cut." He extends that meat hook again and we shake.

Adam Rafferty, P.I. It has a nice ring to it. I can't wait to tell Amy!

THREE

The next morning I walk down Slater street checking the building numbers as I go. It's a quiet area in the downtown where residential brick buildings are losing ground to the encroachment of office and commercial establishments. At number 152, I pause looking up at the large bay windows of a converted Victorian mansion before a small plaque with the name Drogan Investigations catches my eye. An arrow under the letters point to a set of steps leading down to the basement level where his office is located. You'd miss the sign and his office if you weren't looking.

I go down and open the door. A waiting room with a line of metal chairs against one wall and a coffee table scattered with out-of-date magazines greet me. There's also an empty desk where once there was a secretary typing and answering the phone. The door beside opens and Mike fills the frame, a big grin on his face.

"You decided to give it a try, huh?" He nods his head to the side inviting me into the inner sanctum where he works.

"Yeah. But I'm not quitting my delivery job. Not yet anyway." So far, I'm not impressed with what I'm seeing.

Inside his office there's an ancient wooden desk with a laptop, and a heap of file folders stacked neatly next to it. A bank of metal cabinets flank his leather chair while a printer sits waiting in the corner. I take a seat in the chair across the desk from him.

"Not a bad idea. What's your hours there?" He slides a file folder across to me.

"Noon to eight most days. When they're busy, I sometimes have to go in earlier." I reach for the folder but his paw anchors it.

Holding up a separate sheet of paper, he says, "Before we start I need you to sign a privacy disclosure form. Not that you will have much interaction with clients without me being there, but I have to get formal assurance to protect my clients." Again, his eyes examine me closely.

And I check him out as well. Remembering Mike through the yellow haze of the dimly lit bar last night, I can tell he is a straight shooter. He works hard when he works, and while he may push some boundaries he's got his principles. And don't ever try to bullshit him because his BS detector is like sonar. It's all there in front of me.

"Sure. That's not a problem." I sign the form without even reading it. I sit back and wait.

"There's this case I'm working on. A partner in the law firm Wilson, Pratt and Cooke. He's in his fifties. His wife suspects that he may be having an affair. Her sister Mona was recently dumped for a trophy wife, and I've got my suspicions that she may be blowing smoke up Sheila's ass." He makes a small wave with one hand dismissively. "You know, the whole misery loves company kind of thing."

Something doesn't add up. This sounds pretty straightforward. Why would he need my help? "So you've followed him, right? And is there another woman? It would help if I could touch an article of his clothing or an object close to him. Is that what you need from me?"

He sits back watching his fingers, all the while tapping a pen against the desk. "Not yet. But it's strange. Every Tuesday and Thursday for the last few years Anthony has worked late, supposedly at a meeting with the other partners."

"Supposedly. So you know he isn't doing that."

"He leaves work at four, goes to a Philippine restaurant and doesn't leave there till nine at night. The last couple of times I followed him, I went into the restaurant to see what's up. No one spends five hours eating. The building where the restaurant is has a few upper floors. So I think, yeah, that's where he's spending time. Is it a massage parlor? A front for some gambling joint? I couldn't find any entranceway to the upper floors from the restaurant—I managed to check that out." He drums his fingers on the desktop. "But now it gets oddball."

"How?"

"Well, last week I followed him into the restaurant's restroom and he literally vanished. No sign of him even though I'd seen him go in there."

"So what's upstairs in that building?" I got a sense of the place, the cooking smells and chatter from what was ringing around in Mike's head.

"Apartments, from what I could tell from the entrance on the side of the building. I checked out that entranceway, but it's locked up tight. I could see some mailboxes and doorbells." He shrugged. "It looks legit—I don't think there's a gambling joint or brothel up those stairs."

"Why are you sure?"

"No traffic. I spent a full night staking out the entrance of the apartments. Places like bootleg casinos or brothels have people coming and going all the time. The apartment entrance is just where some people live. The place looks a little rough on the outside but inside is a whole different story. From what I could see there's only four apartments, two on each floor. They've got to be huge and the hallway has Berber wool carpets."

"So, somehow he's able to get into one of these places from the restaurant?"

"Something's fishy about the place. And guess what? The

lawyer *owns* the building. It took me a while to track back through the numbered companies, but yeah, it's *owned* by Anthony Wilson." He sits back and crosses his arms over his chest, straining a couple buttons on his white cotton shirt.

"So you want me to go in there? Follow Anthony to the restaurant tonight and try to get a reading on him. See what he's up to." I pull my cell phone out to check the time and get the address of this restaurant. "You have a picture of this guy?"

Mike opens the file folder and flicks a photocopy of a man in his fifties, graying hair, handsome even if his nose was more like a beak. It must be from a newspaper article at some charity event because he's in a tuxedo standing next to a petite blond only a few years younger. Probably his wife, Sheila. I snap a pic with my phone and then stand up.

"I'll case the joint."

Mike snorts a laugh. "You been watching too much TV, Adam." He scoops up the photo and puts it back in the file. "It's out on Counter Street. You can't miss it. It's the only Philippine restaurant in town." He looks sad for a moment. "I seriously hope I've been wrong and that it's some kind of cathouse. Sheila will be heartbroken if he has a mistress."

Mike is giving off genuine fondness for Sheila while at the same time resenting her sister, even though it was Mona who had steered the business his way.

"How much is all this worth to me, Mike? I mean, aside from the pleasure of your company?"

"I charge seventy-five an hour, kid. Let me know how much time you spend. Needless to say, I don't dog it to rack the bill higher. That's not my style." He turns to his laptop already moving on to whatever other cases he has lined up.

This is a trial run for both of us. But I'm getting good vibes that things will work out. "I'll call you later to let you know what I've found. Or maybe I'll see you at The Slip tonight? You can buy me a beer."

"Gladly, if you can get this case off my back. I'd love to find that hidden door in that joint. He's got a slick operation going, whatever it is." Mike is a two-finger typing wizard punching the keys of the computer.

***

After leaving Mike's office, I have some time to kill before I have to go into the delivery job. As I pass by a thrift store, an idea pops into my twisted brain so I duck in. At the back of the store, rack after rack of men's clothing hangs, but it's a hat that I want. And right there on a shelf are a few dark fedora's that don't look like they've seen much use. I pluck the brown one and plop it onto my head. Immediately a sense of grief wafts over me, and I picture the previous owner—some old man who'd worn this at his brother's funeral.

I put it back and grab the other one. That's the problem with buying anything used. Sometimes the karma that comes off the stuff is not right. But the second one, black and in perfect shape is neutral. I picture some skinny guy getting this and being too self conscious to ever wear it.

Eyeing myself in the mirror hanging on the wall I adjust it so that it hangs low over my eyes. I fish my cell phone from my pocket and take a selfie. My thumbs flew texting Amy with the pic.

Adam Rafferty P.I. Specializing in finding lost causes.

I chuckle picturing her face when she gets it.

"Do you need some help?" A middle-aged, black lady scowls at me. "You buying that hat or just being one, as in ass-hat?"

I feel my cheeks warm and notice another patron eyeing me as well. But this guy looks like anything he finds in the store will be a vast improvement to the rags he's got on. "Yeah. I'll take it." I slip the hat off and skulk behind the lady walking to the cash.

I hand her a few dollars and then scurry out of there.

When I walk into Rabbit Express my shoulders slump. Just my luck that Phil is behind the counter, giving Hilda an early lunch break.

He looks up from his iPhone for a moment. "What happened? You fall out of bed or something? You're not due in for another hour."

"It's *you,* Phil. I couldn't wait to see your ugly mug." I walk over to the counter to see the order sheets. Again, luck is with me. An order for a pickup from the wrecker's and deliver to an auto-body shop near that Philippine restaurant. For good measure I grab the second order as well which would keep me out on the road away from the office and Mr. Personality.

"I might as well get these out of the way." I grab the keys to the van and head out the back door. Phil doesn't even bother looking up from the porn site he ogles.

A half hour later I park the van in front of the restaurant and get out. I look up at the rust-colored brick building checking the windows for any sign of life. It's funny but I get impressions of children flitting through my mind—not scared or brutalized, more like *happy* images. This doesn't sit with what Mike said. He's under the impression that the place might be a brothel of some kind.

I go into the restaurant to check it out. A tiny Asian lady rushes over to hand me a menu when I take a table near the window. "Thanks. But I'll just have a coffee."

She smiles and nods while scooping the cutlery up, lest I dirty it with my presence.

"I've never been here before. I'll have to come back for dinner later. I love to try different ethnic foods. Have you been open long?" Already I feel all P.I. and stuff, being chatty to get information.

"Open five year. Yes. Please to come back for dinner. Adobo on special today. Only nine ninety-nine." All the while her head nods like a bobble, and the smile never leaves her dark eyes.

"Sounds great!" I can't help but smile back at her. There's nothing sinister about this woman, only a hard worker who cherishes her family. I sense a son and daughter in college that she's very proud of.

She walks away, and I take that opportunity to check out this restroom where the client's husband has given Mike the slip. The restaurant isn't all that busy considering it's close to noon. A few tables are occupied with older Philippine people who look like friends. This is their daily routine stopping by for lunch. The aroma of garlic makes my mouth water when a waft leaves the open door of the kitchen. Another server appears carrying plates of food.

The men's room is nothing special. Just a few urinals, three stalls and sinks. I pop into each stall looking for anything that would indicate a doorway. But of course, it probably isn't easy to spot and who would want to have to slide by a toilet to get out anyway? I tap along each of the two wood-paneled walls, but there's nothing hollow sounding or suspicious. But still I get a feeling, and it's not just the rough grain under my fingers. It's an awareness of anticipation, a feeling of love that the last person who touched this wall experienced.

If this Anthony guy managed to give Mike the slip, it had to be from some catch in this wall that opens up to the other part of the building. But damned if I can find it. This is going to take meeting the guy for me to figure this out. There are clues but not enough to find that final piece.

I wash my hands and then hightail it back to my table where a steaming cup of coffee awaits. I'm barely seated when my cell phone buzzes with a text.

Go to 571 Oakley Lane for a pickup, and take it to Art Alter Gallery on Main.

Of course I know the gallery, but I have to do a search for this Oakley Lane I've never heard of. Great. It's going to take me out about five miles into the countryside according to the map. I still have a couple of stops to drop off the other items. But there's no way I want to miss seeing this lawyer when he comes to this restaurant at four.

I gulp the coffee and leave a finsky on the table. Yup. A finsky. With my hat and work with Drogan, I'm getting all Phillip Marlow. Sue me, sweetheart. When I leave the building the sound of children's laughter in the schoolyard down the street fills the warm springtime air. I pause and look up at the building above the restaurant. Someone in that building has kids that go to that same school down the block from me. It comes to me in a flash and I know it's true. The place isn't a brothel like Mike suspected.

Not. At. All.

I get in the van and program the phone's GPS for Oakley Lane. The Android woman on the phone practically purrs when she speaks, giving me sexy directions, taking me to the outskirts of town to this Oakley Lane place. Hell, hearing her voice is a welcome distraction. The way my luck's been going, it's probably the only sexy voice I'm likely to ever hear, so yeah, it makes me smile.

Stands of trees bordering the two lane road show the undeniable march of spring with leaves bursting from their buds, peppering the branches. Two more miles of farms and fields follow before I see the sign I'm looking for.

"You're here, big boy. Come and get it." The phone's sultry robot purrs.

Chuckling I flip the app off. It would have been nice if Jane or Jasmine had said that last night instead of hurrying out of the bar like I'd grown a second head.

The lane isn't paved, and I have to swerve to avoid potholes that threaten to swallow the van. Large oak trees border the cow-path drive like sentries. A flock of crows take flight darkening the meager sunlight that manages to filter through. There aren't any houses besides the one up ahead that looms, a three-story, stone monstrosity with upper windows akin to the multi-lenses of a fly, watching my progress.

The hair on the back of my neck tingles as I stop the van. The warmth of the day can't shake the shiver that tightens my shoulders. The only time I've ever felt this way about a house was when I was twelve and had stumbled onto the Donnelly house property.

That day scared the shit out of me.

FOUR

That day was seven years ago; I was just twelve years old. It had been a warm spring day, much like the one today. That morning I raced out of the house in time to see the yellow school bus at the end of the block on its way to school leaving me in the faint exhaust smoke. I was left with a choice. Skipping school would throw my parents into a conniption and I'd be grounded for a week, or I could suck it up and walk.

I pulled the knapsack strap higher on my shoulder and set off down the street. As I passed by a vacant lot it occurred to me that the school wasn't that far away as the crow flies. It would mean cutting through a ravine and stand of trees, but I'd chop the walking time in half. And if it wasn't too hard walking it would allow me to grab an extra fifteen minutes of sleep each morning.

A bonus on top of the extra sleep was that I wouldn't have to deal with Ralph Bufford on the bus ride. He and his buddies picked on me the entire ride to school. Every day, all year long I'd been the target of their teasing. Well, it started with teasing, but by that morning they were starting to shove me around when the driver wasn't looking. A crappy way to start your day, right? I squared my shoulders. To hell with catching the bus, getting picked on by that bully, Ralph, and his gang of thugs.

After crossing the scrubby lot, the land dipped down, and I had to grab at the branches of mangy cedar trees to keep from slipping in the muddy spots. At the bottom of the ravine, the trees became larger and more plentiful. As I threaded my way through the wooded copse the sound of water gurgling made me pause. To my right was a small stream that followed the same direction where I needed to go to get to school.

A splash in the water got my curiosity going and I headed over to check it out. In an eddy of water pooled and swirling slightly before trickling over a flat rock was a dark fish. He hovered just below the surface. I watched him for a few seconds before he skirted to the side and flew up, landing in the flow of the stream a couple feet away. The sunlight reflected a ribbon of pink going along his side when he'd been in the air. A rainbow trout!

I raced after him, my eyes never leaving his thin body and the swirl of water in his wake. Time, school, everything was forgotten as I skipped along, pouncing from rock to rock in pursuit of the fish. I never noticed the deadly quiet as I went deeper and deeper into the woods. Not even a cheep from birds or crickets, only the gurgling sound of the brook.

It emptied into a pool about twelve feet across, darker and with depth to it that made finding the fish harder.

"Adam."

I jerked and then spun around to see the source of the voice. My heart just about stopped when I saw the house.

Oh my God, I'd stumbled onto the Donnelly place. Even without hearing all the horror stories about the serial killer who once lived there, I'd known that it was a bad place. Seeing it from the safety of my parents' car I'd felt a malevolent presence watching me as we drove by.

And now it was about thirty feet away. Somehow I'd landed in the backyard of the cursed manse.

"Aaadaaam." A girl's soft voice called in a singsong way

that sent a shiver down my spine.

She stepped onto the back veranda and my jaw fell open. She was a vision of beauty right out of a fairy tale, elegant and lovely in a frothy, white dress. Raven hair hung to her waist and her eyes, even from this distance, showed an azure blue next to milk-white skin. She was the most gorgeous creature I'd ever laid eyes on.

"Adam? Come closer. Let's play a game."

My feet started moving, pushing through the long, matted grass as I fell into her smile, my focus only on her. My foot was on the bottom step before a wave of nausea and sense of foreboding overcame me. I stopped short. The air around me wavered like the shimmering heat waves above tarmac on a hot day in July. The stench of sewer gas filtered into my nostrils.

"ADAM! Come here!" She morphed right before my eyes! Her ivory skin darkened and her eyes glowed red. Even her lustrous hair transformed into writhing snakes, and the white dress was replaced with scales dripping a yellow ooze as she grew in size. Towering over me, she... IT bellowed, "COME TO ME!"

As I recoiled back in horror, this *thing* lashed out like a striking serpent with glinting, yellow talons.

"I MARK YOU, BOY!"

A searing, hot pain ripped through my thigh! Gasping, I fell on my ass. I skittered backward, desperately trying to scramble to my feet. My back pack fell away as I ran through the yard, the grass tugging at my legs to ensnare me. The hair on the back of my neck spiked high as I looked for the stream.

It wasn't there!

Only the trees with twisted dark limbs that looked like arms and hands reaching to get me.

The laughter that blared from the house shot a jolt of fear up my spine. It held the hysterical ring of many voices, some young as children, some old as time—and all dripping with malice.

It was only later, racing through the forest that the chilling wetness registered. I had actually peed myself. If only that were the worst of it.

When I peeled my jeans away in the bathroom at home, three red gashes crossed my thigh. They weren't deep enough for stitches but they hurt like hell. I still have the faint lines there, where I'd been clawed by that…thing.

I'd had lots of encounters with spirits, but never, ever had I seen a demon. And what lived in the Donnelly house was surely that. A demon who had marked me.

Needless to say, I never went back. I never missed the school bus ever again. Ralph Bufford and his buddies were nothing compared to what I had encountered.

***

Shaking my head to clear it of the dark memory, I get out of the van slowly, my eyes taking in every nook and cranny, the sides of the building and the walkway to the large veranda. I can't shake the feeling that something watches me. And it's definitely a *something* not a someone. The pervading sense of déjà vu makes my blood run cold.

I've hardly stepped up to the door when it creaks open. A middle-aged woman stands there, her gaze hard, peering at me as her fingers clutch the edge of the door.

"You here for the package?" Even her voice is sharp and metallic.

"Yeah. Rabbit Express. You need something delivered to the art gallery, right? Where is it?" I stand a couple feet away from the door, out of arm's reach. No matter what, I'm not going in that house. Every fiber of my body screams at me to run back to the van and boot it out the drive. And that same nausea I felt at the Donnelly house is rising in the back of my throat, sour in my mouth.

The door opens wider still and a draft seeps out. It's rank, like sewer gas. There's a large statue on the floor wrapped in layers of bubble-wrap, sitting next to a staircase.

She points to it with a bony finger. "There it is. It's pretty heavy. Mind you don't bang it when you put it in your vehicle." The woman exudes a dark aura, which adds to my discomfort.

How is she even alive with this much sickness inside her? And as for the package, there's no way I'm touching it. I don't want to know anything about it. I get the feeling that holding it would be like breathing anthrax.

"Sorry. If you want that delivered you'll have to put it in my van. Better yet, if you're worried it could get damaged, call the gallery and have them send someone out." I'm already edging back toward the stairs.

"Adam? Is that *you,* Adam Rafferty?"

A shot of fear turns my bowels into water. I *know* that voice. It's the same one I heard at the Donnelly house!

The middle-aged woman is nowhere to be seen. Instead, the figure from my childhood is back, standing in the center of the doorframe. It's an older version of the girl I saw that day. Her hair is pitch-black, swept up in a messy bun, and her eyes have that same azure glaze as she did that day. And again, belying the fact that her soul is black as sin, she wears a gauzy, white robe. So sheer that the darkness of protruding nipples can be seen, the swell of her hips and long, supple thighs.

Again, it's like I've been caught in a spider web, unable to think, betrayed by my raging hormones as I stand mesmerized. I can't look away even though I know I should.

"I knew our paths would cross again." The creature's gaze slithers down my body, lingering for a few beats on my groin which aches with sudden lust. A smile curls her scarlet lips. "You're not a boy any longer. I've waited for this."

The beast thing practically floats over to where I stand. I'm stock-still as she bends her head to me. The wave of pure pleasure that pulses from her lips brushing mine is electric, searing every cell in my body. Any wish I had of leaving evaporates with her kiss. I'm lost in the bliss of this moment.

When her fingers slide across my thigh where she marked me before, I totally lose it. The pleasure cascading through me, makes my body shake and I gasp, barely able to stay upright. My mind has short-circuited, totally blank while my body sways on leaden feet.

Her whisper is sickeningly assured, "I knew I'd see you

again. The next time we meet, three will be the charm."

She leans in again and her tongue, wet and swollen, slides along my lips.

In that instant my senses return and I jerk back, raising my hand to swipe at my mouth and spit. When I look over to her, she's gone.

It all happened so quickly that I wonder for a moment if it happened at all. But the odor lingering and the foul taste in my mouth are proof it did.

"Well? What are you waiting for? That package won't deliver itself." The other woman stands in the doorway glaring at me.

"Forget it, lady! I'm outta here!" I race down the steps and over to the van. Why had I lingered when I heard that demon's voice? I should have run as fast as my feet could carry me, like I'd done back at the Donnelly place.

Stones and dirt kick up after the van as I wheel it down the laneway. I'm fleeing evil, yet I can't shake the sinking dread that part of that unearthly beast lingers inside me. It touched me, kissed me, and for a fleeting moment I'd actually liked it. I had been completely under its spell, betrayed by my hormones. And it knew my weakness; it had been eagerly waiting for this time.

Its words—"The next time we meet three will be the charm"—still resonates darkly. The creature is a magnet that attracts and repulses at the same time.

FIVE

Still shaky as hell, I ignore the cell phone buzzing for the third time. I know it's Hilda, and she's had a call from that lady about her art pickup. Too bad. The only thing I want more than to forget that episode is to take a shower, a scalding hot one to wash away all memories of that evil entity.

If only I could.

It's hard to shake the horror of that creature but I have to. Every time I picture her; her kiss and the stench, my gut churns and I gag. This isn't the time nor place for a purge of that nature. And yet, at the same time a deep, throbbing, lusting desire niggles deep inside.

I give my head a shake and still my brain, focusing on reading street signs and store names as I drive through the small city.

When I finish the other pickups and deliveries it's just about four in the afternoon—the time that I need to be at the restaurant to catch the philandering lawyer. Believe me, doing this job for Mike is a lifesaver keeping thoughts of that evil thing I encountered submerged.

I park as far away from the door to the restaurant as I can, while still being able to keep an eye out for him.

Right on schedule he wheels a gray BMW in the spot next to me. If I'm trying to blend into the background, so is he. When he gets out I size him up, getting a reading on his aura. I go over him, up and down with my sidey-eyes. It doesn't make sense. People who exude pink are generally loyal and trustworthy with strong moral values, not prone to slinking around with a mistress on the side.

I'm right on his heels going into the restaurant. The lady who served me earlier rushes over to greet him, even giving him a one-armed hug. Instead of taking a table, Anthony makes a beeline for the men's room. I have to wave the waitress off as I follow him across the room. So much for discretion.

When he hears the door open he pauses and then steps over to the urinal to use it. Waves of impatience roll off him, waiting for me to leave but that's exactly what I'm not about to do—not until I get more information.

I go past him to the next urinal and fake a stumble. It's awkward at best, but I manage to graze his shoulder with my hand as I regain my balance.

In that instant I see into his head. A picture of two children, a boy about six and a younger girl, flash in my head. It's genuine love that he feels for them. His children? There's a woman, the mother, but the only feeling in his heart for her is fondness. This visit isn't about anything sexual, it's a *family* visit. His glance at the wall where I suspect the door is, tells me everything in that moment.

"Excuse me. Sorry. Must be a loose tile on the floor that tripped me," I mumble and then take a spot at the farthest urinal.

"No problem," he murmurs, turning back to the task at hand.

I decide to go out on a limb even though this is my first case working for Mike. "Say? Aren't you Anthony Wilson? I saw your picture in the newspaper. You were at a charity dinner with your wife... Sheila?"

This time he looks me in the eye as he zips his trousers. For an instant suspicion and guilt play tug-of-war in his wide eyes.

"Yeah. I didn't think kids your age read anything except what's on the internet, let alone the society pages of the *Herald*." He washes his hands, glancing over at me, waiting for a reply.

I've pushed my luck, and he knows I'm up to something. "My boss pointed it out. She reads the newspapers. MS research is something she's passionate about, and of course that was the fundraiser, right? Your wife looked pretty, so that helps me remember too."

He turns, continuing to scrub his hands. "Yeah. Thanks."

As I stand at the sink next to him, scenes and feelings pour from his mind. Taking the two kids to the park, playing hide-and-seek with them, helping them with their homework. Funny though, there's a thick layer of guilt underlying it, a flash of his wife sitting at home waiting while he spends time with his second family.

I finish in the bathroom and hurry out. Let the guy slip through that hidden door without me hanging around holding him up. It might be his last time to enjoy his children and his secret life before everything falls apart for him.

Mike never told me how shitty and complicated this job could get. But that's life, right?

SIX

Later that night when I enter the bar I see Mike hunched at a table in the corner, nursing a glass of beer. He signals to the bartender for another round and then beckons me over to join him.

"Hey Mike." I slide into the seat across from him and wait for the drink to arrive before opening up about the case.

"Well? Did you get a bead on him?" Mike sits back holding the glass before his mouth, and his gaze explores my face.

"Yeah. You were right about there being a secret doorway in that bathroom." The next part needs a quick swallow of liquid courage. I take a deep gulp and put the glass on the table. "But it's not what you think he's up to. There's another woman all right—"

"Aw, shit."

"Let me finish, okay? He's got another *family*, Mike." I watch his eyes narrow.

"It's worse than I thought. The two-timing bastard."

"No. Look, the guy desperately wanted kids, but he

couldn't have them with Sheila. He made an arrangement with a Philippine woman. He brought her here and had two children with her. Twice a week he sees them. He covers all their expenses." I can still feel the guy's anguish over what this would do to his wife if it ever got out. Much as I hate telling on the lawyer, this was why Mike hired me.

"So, this has been going on for some time. If not for Mona putting a bug in Sheila's ear this may never have surfaced." He blows out a resigned sigh through pursed lips, setting the glass down softly.

He doesn't like this any more than I do. I lean forward, pleading this stranger's case. "It's wrong, I know. But he saved that woman from a shitty life, man. It sucks over there, especially for poor, uneducated women." I shake my head slowly from side to side, recalling Wilson's thoughts about the mother of his kids. "She might have ended up in prostitution if she'd stayed in the Philippines. And he has two children that he's nuts about. He's also crazy about Sheila."

"So, what do you think I should do, Adam? Lie to Sheila? Cover this up?"

"I don't know. You're the boss. Your decision, not mine, I'm afraid." I pick at the label of the beer bottle. "He knew what I was doing talking to him in the bathroom. He's been expecting someone to find out sooner or later, and presto, I enter the picture."

Mike looks like he's lost his best friend. It isn't so much feeling for the guy but rather knowing how hurt the wife is gonna be. Telling her this news will take a piece out of Mike.

When the door opens I look at the mirror behind the bar. The movie next door has ended right on time. A pretty redhead followed by two other people, a mousy brunette and a guy in his late twenties, walk in. When they take seats at the bar I can't believe my luck. The brunette and the guy are an item, the two of them sitting close, and there's an empty seat next to the redhead.

"Hey Mike, don't take it personally but you're not my type. But that fox at the bar *is*. So..." I get up, never taking my eyes off her reflection in the mirror.

"Good luck, kid." He leans over to get a better look at her. "You're definitely going to need it. You're punching above your weight there, Adam. Maybe *I* should go over."

"Yeah, right. She's young enough to be your daughter, you letch." I look at him for a moment when an image of a blond girl, pigtails flying out as she swings high in the air, forms in his head. "You have a daughter, don't you?"

"Yeah. She'd make that girl at the bar seem young too." His eyes take on a faraway look and waves of sadness cloud him.

"When's the last time you saw Mary-Jane?"

For a moment he looks surprised I know her name, but then the hardened glaze is back in his eyes. "A long time. That's another story that I don't want to get into now. You'd better make tracks, Romeo, or someone's gonna beat you to that empty bar stool."

I give him a two-fingered salute and leave it at that, wandering over, trying my best to act nonchalant as I slip in beside her. One thing Mike is definitely right about is the fact that she's out of my league. She could have stepped off the cover of *Cosmo* magazine. But with the orange-hued waves hovering over a slender body, I actually might have a decent shot at this.

She turns slightly and smiles at me before resuming the conversation with the brunette and her boyfriend. Just that friendly smile makes the breath in my chest hitch. God. Forget *Cosmo*; she could model for *Playboy*! Cynthia... her name comes to me in a jolt. But it's weird. I get images usually, but this is a voice blaring in my head.

"Excuse me." I'm about to ask her what she thought of '*The Big Lebowski'* movie when the voice in my head stops me cold. '*Don't ask her that! Try something original.*'

She turns, and her brown eyes dance with amusement. "Yes?"

My cheeks flame a little as I scramble for something witty or engaging to say. But words fail me. Then the whisper comes again, '*Her perfume, idiot!*'

"I love that perfume you're wearing! It's Poivre by Caron, right?" Thankfully the name flashed in her mind at the mention of perfume.

"Yeah. How'd you know?" She's genuinely surprised, flashing a wide smile, mentally congratulating herself that the knockoff she bought was worth it. She turns into me, inviting more conversation.

'*It was your girlfriend's favorite perfume. She was wearing it the night she died. Try to look sad.*' Again the words whisper in my mind and then leap off my tongue as I do my best to be the picture of sorrow. The words leave my lying tongue before I can even give it a sober second thought.

"Awww... I'm so sorry." She slumps and her hand pats my arm. Immediately I know all about her—she works with small kids. She's' kind, sensitive, and more important to me, hasn't dated anyone in months.

Just as I'm about to change the subject before this lie gets any bigger, the voice again stops me, '*Tell her you haven't been with anyone since the death of your girlfriend.*' What the hell? Where's this coming from? This isn't my style. At. All.

My voice betrays my reticence, going on auto-pilot. "Thanks. Amanda was everything to me. I haven't dated a soul since... well since—"

"Oh, you poor guy."

'*Adam. Tell her your name, idiot.*' "I'm Adam." I can feel her sympathy and... dare I even hope— interest? This is baffling, but.... good?

Her hand still rests on my arm radiating warmth. "I'm Cynthia Brooks." She glances at my beer and then shoots a shy smile. "Can I buy you a drink?"

There's more coming through than just that question. Cynthia's hoping to be the one to pull me out of my blue funk, the showstopper who can *fix* me. The voice again comes through, gloating, '*See? Play hard to get for once in your miserable life.*'

"Thanks, but no. I'll buy you and your friends a round and then I really should split. I'm afraid I'm not great company. This is the anniversary of Amanda's..." That one just came to me on my own... I think.

"No way! I insist. Especially not on *this night* of all nights. That painful loss. You shouldn't be alone." Her hand slips from my arm, and she leans closer, slipping her fingers onto my thigh.

I should feel guilty but I don't for some odd reason. This girl thinks she's helping me. Who am I to deprive her of that joy? I give her a forlorn smile and cover her hand with mine. "You're really sweet."

Sam, the bartender is watching this with wide eyes. He never thought he'd live to see the day that I'd actually walk out of this bar with a girl. And not just any girl, but a total knockout.

She turns to her friends and introduces me to them, "Haley and Andrew, this is Adam."

I lean over and shake both their hands, murmuring the polite '"pleased to meet you."' The voice once more sears through my head. *'Go to the bathroom. It'll be a cinch that she'll tell them your sad story when you're gone. You're killing it, Adam!'*

"I'm sorry. I'll be right back." I'm kind of shell-shocked when I get to my feet, but I stop at Mike's table before heading to the men's room. "I've got a lock on this one! Can you believe that?"

He looks at me, then across to Cynthia and back to me. "Well, I'll be damned."

"Watch and learn, old man." I swagger a little going over to the bathroom, taking my time. That voice. It told me what to do, what to say and it is spot on. For once, I won't be sleeping alone. What's a few little white lies?

As I wash my hands I glance into the mirror. The funny thing about seeing auras is that I can never see my own. That is, until tonight. There's a darkness emanating from me and I jerk back, my stomach roiling.

It hits me like a wall. That voice whispering in my head. There had been a hint of familiarity to it, but I 'didn't want to acknowledge it when I am doing so well with Cynthia, spinning the web of lies.

Oh God.

The evil spirit I encountered when I was twelve at the Donnelly house. And again earlier today... It's here now.

Somehow, it has stuck itself on to me! And now it's coaching me? Helping me suck this poor girl in with a total bullshit story? Preying on her kindness, like a total jerk?

I finish in the washroom and don't even look over at her as I race from the bar. This isn't who I am. I'm not a liar. Maybe a few fibs to spare someone's feelings but nothing conniving like this. I certainly would never knowingly use people in this way. It's this *thing* in my head.

"Get out!" I tear at my hair, racing down the street like a crazed maniac.

But can I shake this thing that has somehow attached itself to me?

SEVEN

When I get home, I'm shaking from the run and the dread that this entity is inside me, manipulating me. Thank God, my roomie has gone to bed. I need to be alone to figure this out.

It had that girl eating out of my palm with its lies, directing me with vile whispers inside my head. If not for what happened earlier today and then seeing that dark shadow hovering over me in the bathroom mirror, I might have gone along with it. How had it done this? Is this the "'third time's the charm'" it warned me about?

But more important for now is the need to find a way to get rid of it inside me. I want nothing to do with this thing, ever. I grab my laptop and then hunker down onto the bed to research this. Surely the internet will help me.

I cruise the sites that talk about demons and possession, but the cases all seem to be similar to what I'd seen when I watched '*The Exorcist*'. This isn't what it's like for me at all. This wraith isn't twisting my head in a full circle or spewing vomited pea soup; it's playing on my weakness, which is wanting to get laid.

Nothing noble about it, but I'm almost nineteen. What would you expect?

There are sites on cleansing with sage smudges and wearing protective crystals. Maybe I need to try that, even though it seems too simplistic to actually work.

Praying, getting a blessing from a priest? The only times I ever went to church were at Christmas and Easter. Somehow, I think an all-knowing God will recognize my self-serving sudden interest and laugh up his sleeve. What a hypocrite I would be.

Maybe my best bet is to ignore it. It whispers in my ear—so what? I don't have to listen to it, do I? And it only showed up when I was trying to pick up that poor girl. I can control this. At least until I find how to banish it.

I set the laptop aside and then get up to brush my teeth. Avoiding glancing in the mirror I try to think of anything else than what happened at that house, meeting the demon again and... No! No. And no.

The lawyer and his second family—that's it. What is going to be the upshot of that?

But the demon slithers in the dark corners of my mind, making my skin crawl. I spit the toothpaste again and again, gagging when I recall the feel of that thing's tongue sliding over my lips. I cling to the edge of the sink to keep from staggering to the side.

This has to stop. But there's nothing I can do about it right now. I need sleep. It's been a day. I'll figure all of this out tomorrow.

***

The hiss of running water followed by a bang niggle in my ears, but I tug the warm blanket higher wanting to fall back into the dream state. I roll over, tugging the extra pillow over my ears trying to get back to that peaceful bliss. But my mind surfaces, bubbling with thoughts that prevent a relapse.

It seems I just got to sleep and now it's time to get up? One eye creaks open and there's light sneaking in between the slats of the blinds on my window. Yanking the comforter higher there's a draft on my lower back.

What the hell? I'm totally nude? Where are the T-shirt and PJ bottoms I put on before going to bed? The added warmth of my T-shirt and flannel pants are ingrained in my nightly ritual, so I *know* I put them on.

When I try to sit up a searing burn in my abdomen makes me flinch. I look down at my gut. Holy shit! Three fresh red welts run from my left nipple crossing my stomach to the hip bone on the other side.

The lines are tender, slightly raised and rough. What the hell? There's even a smear of blood on the comforter from the cuts... like deep cat scratches.

Fragments of a dream pulse in my mind and I freeze. The redhead from the bar played a starring role in what could only be described as a triple X-rated porn flick. My heart pounds hard, and I don't know whether it's from the erotic images flooding my head or the horror that it might actually have been true. Was it? Why am I naked, and what's with the cuts on my gut?

No. No. No.

I shake my head, glancing over at my laptop for confirmation. I ran out of that bar and came home *alone*. Plus, there's got to be a record in my browsing history on the computer. I brushed my teeth, changed into my PJ pants and T-shirt and went to bed *alone*. I know I did.

My chin drops and I look at the angry welts crossing my stomach again. Shit! This isn't the first time I've gotten three scratches like that! On my thigh when I was twelve, that thing marked me at the Donnelly house. And then encountering it again yesterday...

Oh my God. It was with me at the bar feeding lies to that girl and... last night. Somehow that *thing* was here in my room with me last night. I gag at the horror of the next image slinking through my brain. That *thing* and I had sex... wild monkey sex. It's too disgusting to contemplate even for someone like me, a walking hormone. My skin itches threatening to crawl off and slink onto the floor. That sewage-filled she-monster violated my body in a horrid, intimate way.

My body shrinks, folding in, clutching the blankets like a shield and I shudder. I thought I could control this spirit by ignoring it. But it had come to me at night when I was asleep... or at least should have been asleep. If I were honest with myself, it had even exerted its influence in the bar with Cynthia, playing on my weakness. What the hell am I going to do?

At the tap on my door, I almost jump out of my skin.

"Adam? You okay, man?"

It's only Doug, thank God. I get up and scoop the PJ bottoms from the floor, yanking them on before opening the door a crack. "Yeah. I'm fine. Why?"

He does a theatrical eye roll. "The noises man. I thought you were dying in here last night, with all the moaning and groaning. You sick or something?"

My cheeks flame but my brain scrambles for something plausible. "Yeah. I ate some super-hot buffalo wings last night. Note to self. Never again. Sorry it bothered you."

"No problem. There's medicine for acid reflux in the cabinet if you want it." He's already edging away down the hall.

I look around the room and see more evidence of down-and-dirty mayhem. The lampshade is skewed to the side, and the sheets are in a ball bunched at the bottom corner of the bed. There's even a faint odor like a backed-up toilet. Yuck.

My gut clenches making me rush to the bathroom, barely making it before acrid bile spews from my mouth.

When I straighten, and move to the sink a dark shadow flits across the surface of the mirror above it. I jerk back staring after it. But as quick as it appeared there's no trace of it now. Still, I'm filled with a lingering dread that it's close, even though I can't see it. And it left its mark on me. Again.

My hands dry-scrub my face tugging the skin down as I remember its words. "Three's the charm". Charm? *For whom?*

And as for that romp in my room last night, I'd join a Tibetan Monastery before I'd go through *that* again. I turn the shower on and slip my PJ's off. It's a long, long time, before I'm able to leave the hot spray.

Still shaking a little, when I get dressed for the day, my cell phone buzzes with a text. It's Amy checking in, between classes. I put the phone down, not bothering to even read her message. It would be sacrilegious or something connecting with her after what happened last night. This thing taints me, and until I can figure out how to shake it, there's no way I'd risk contaminating Amy. She's way too good a person for that to happen.

EIGHT

"Why me?" I say out loud as I wait for the traffic light to change. Unlike in the bar last night, this fiend is strangely silent. "Did you wear yourself out messing me up, you sick worm!" I get a strange look from a young mother pushing a stroller and she speeds up as she passes. But what does that matter? If she knew why I'm muttering to myself, she'd *run* to get away from me.

'Why not you is a better question, Adam.'

Its voice shocks me and I freeze. But it's not finished.

'You're a perfect specimen to use. Especially with your talents. It's going to be a wild ride, experiencing everything...the taste of chocolate, feeling people's fear, their greed...' A low chuckle echoes in my mind. *'And ohhh… their lust.'*

"Leave me out of your sick schemes, you demented creep! Isn't there some psychopath you'd rather haunt?" I can feel its smile, gloating that it's in my head, and I can't do anything about it.

My jaw clenches so hard my teeth hurt. This thing marked me and then molested me last night. This has got to end right here—right now. "No! You aren't in control. I have free will and I don't accept you in my life. Get lost, cretin!"

The light changes and I cross, heading for Mike's office. I've got to stop thinking about this entity. The only thing I'm accomplishing is giving it credibility and power over me. Not to mention the fact that it's creeping the hell out of me at the same time. It probably likes that, feeding off my fear like a bloodsucker.

Yeah. Talking to Mike and trying my best to act normal is my best move right now. There might be another case he's got lined up that will take my mind off my situation, at least for a while. It's not true, that old saying that if you laid your troubles out on a table along with everyone else's problems and had to choose from the pile, you'd pick your own in a heartbeat. Not me. I'd even take that lawyer's predicament over this entity that's latched on to me.

When my cell phone buzzes again, I sigh. I know it's Amy. She's worried and not answering her will add to that. I pull it from my pocket and read.

What's up? How come you never texted back? Are you okay?

My thumb flies over the keyboard.

Just busy is all. I've been doing this detective gig. TTYL.

I pocket the phone and go down to Mike's hole-in-the-wall office. He's just setting his phone down on the desk when I enter. From the strained tightness in his lips, whatever that call was about wasn't good. "Hey Mike. What's up?"

"I could ask you the same thing. What the hell happened to you last night? Just when it looks like your luck changes, you tear out of the bar like your ass is on fire." He pulls himself up from the leather chair and walks over to the coffeemaker. As he pours he glances over. "Coffee?"

"Sure." I take a seat in the chair across from him. "Something came up that I had to deal with." It's not a lie, but he doesn't need to know the whole story either. There's no doubt in my mind, 'he'll think I am losing my mind. Maybe I am.

As he hands me a mug of black coffee, he snorts. "Must have been something real important to leave in such a hurry."

He thinks I chickened out at the last minute. It's there in the skepticism in his eyes as well as his thoughts. He's right that I bolted, but not for the reason he projects.

"So have you decided what to do about the lawyer and Sheila? That *was* who you were talking to when I came in?" I take a sip of the bitter drink and grimace. It tastes like it was brewed yesterday.

Easing his girth down into the chair, Mike's eyebrows raise almost to his hairline. "Actually, 'I've made up my mind to keep it from her. Why put her through it when obviously it's been fine for the past few years? If he was gonna leave her, he would have done that already. Not everyone's life fits the cookie cutter. Who am I to pass judgment?"

"I sense a 'but' coming." I' already pick up on what he is about to say, but I let him finish.

"The thing is, her husband came clean with everything last night." He runs his hand through his scalp, and there's a rueful smile on his face. "It's funny. People can still surprise me sometimes. Anthony couldn't live with the guilt. But the shocker was her reaction." He shakes his head. "After she got over the hurt, she wanted to meet them—the kids. They think Anthony's their godfather and now *she* wants to be their godmother."

Mike sits back and clasps his hands together over his paunch, his smile spreading, "And if you can believe this—she was hurt he kept this secret from her. It put a wedge between them. She regrets being shut out and not seeing his kids grow."

Whoa. "That's a special kind of woman in my books. If my father did this to my mother, she'd kill him." I picture my no-nonsense mother. On second thought, she'd castrate him before she killed him. My father would never dream of cheating on her. They might not be overly affectionate but there was a deep love and respect there.

'Besides, she had Seth and Amy. No need for the old man to sow any more wild seeds.' I jerk forward, slopping some of the hot coffee on my lap. Shit! That voice in my head... It's' back!

"You okay, Adam?" Mike peers at me and then grabs some tissues from the box on his desk, tossing them over to sop up the wetness. "You look like you got a sudden cramp or something."

"No... no, I'm fine." I dab my jeans and then set the mug on his desk. "Look, I'm glad that it worked out for her, y'know. But I actually stopped in to see if there was any more work you wanted me to do." Anything that snags my attention so that the voice can't get through would be great.

"Well..." He looks down at his desk, his fingers fiddling with a pen.

He's embarrassed? Hell, I'll take whatever job he's got lined up. I've got to stay busy, get my mind on other things besides this horrible thing I encountered yesterday. I hate the fact that I fell into its twisted spell last night and the fact that it's still tracking me. I have to be stronger than it is. And if that means working harder, I'm all over that one.

"Come on. Out with it." But even before he speaks I know what he's about to say. I can see why he's reluctant to take this case on. "A lost dog? Seriously?"

His head jerks up and he sputters, "Not just *any* dog, Adam. Chauncy is an English bulldog, a pedigree with a family tree that would put the royal family to shame. He's worth ten thousand bucks."

"Who would pay that kind of money for a mutt? Especially a dog that butt ugly." With all the wrinkles and jowls bulldogs are so homely they're actually kind of cute. Amy would love him to death.

"The owner is willing to pay us three thousand smackeroos to get him back. She's beside herself about losing him. She let him out first thing this morning so he could do his business. When she called him, fifteen minutes later, he was gone. The yard is completely fenced, so someone had to have snatched him."

"Do you think there'll be a ransom note?" Even though it really isn't all that funny I can't stop the chuckle, picturing a dark alley, the dog being exchanged for a briefcase full of unmarked bills.

"Look, do you want to help me out or not? I figure if you touch something that was close to Chauncy, like his bed or leash you might pick up on where he is." Mike sits back, folding his arms over his chest.

"I see. I'm your psychic bloodhound. Pretty fitting in this case." It's kind of fun giving him a hard time, watching him squirm a bit. This is quite a come down from when he'd been a police detective.

"Something like that." He scowls, pulling himself up from the chair. "Let's take a run over to the lady's house. We can be in and out of there in half an hour." He leads the way out of the office, setting the lock on the door behind him.

"I have to be at the delivery job at one. Think you can drop me off there when we finish the great dognapping heist?"

"Keep it up with the smart mouth, and you'll talk yourself right out of this job, kid." He stops next to a vintage caddy and throws me a final warning scowl before getting in.

On the drive to the outskirts of the town, Mike's pretty quiet. It might be time to ease up with the teasing so I offer up a bone. "My sister Amy always brings stray mongrels home. There were times when it was like living in an animal shelter. Not that I minded. All kidding aside, I actually like dogs. I can understand this woman being busted up about losing her mutt."

He looks over at me. "Your sister sounds nice. Is she like you? I mean with this psychic radar thing?"

"No. But she's the kindest girl you'll ever meet. I miss her a lot." It's tempting to get my phone out and send her a text but I'll wait till later. I'll take a pic of me and the ten-thousand-dollar dog and send it. She'll like that.

"Where are your folks? I mean what happened that you left home?" His glance is nonchalant but I know he's listening carefully.

"They're back in Buffalo. I got tired of the constant nagging. I've got an older brother Seth, who shits gold, and Amy... well, she's pretty well perfect too. I never really fit in with them nor anything else for that matter."

"Have you always had this 'gift'? That would have made school tough, I imagine."

I look out the side window remembering the times I was beat up by the bullies at school. Even in kindergarten the other kids had picked up on the fact that I wasn't like them. And when you're young, being different is the last thing you want.

"Yeah. School was no walk in the park. And yes, I was born with this, like my granny. She used to talk to me about it. She warned me against telling people the things I see but hey... you know me."

"Snatching defeat out of the jaws of victory. Yeah I've seen you at work in the bar." He flips the turn signal on and pulls into a driveway bordered by lawns that could shame a golf course.

The house is huge and perfect. Everything outside is elegant and perfectly displayed. A birdbath is set on the lawn and is spotless; at the end of the walkway are two cast-iron chairs that have never been sat in, judging from the perfect lawn below them. It's more like a museum than a home. I follow Mike up the granite steps and wait as he pushes the doorbell. We're quite the pair of professionals. Him in a suit that's way past its 'best before' date and me in scruffy jeans and a Pearl Jam T-shirt.

The door opens and a dark-haired woman in an oversized blouse and yoga pants stands there. Her grief and worry is palpable even if you didn't notice bloodshot eyes and a red nose from all the tears she's shed.

"Lisa Jefferson? I'm Mike Drogan. We spoke on the phone this morning." He casts a glance at me, "This is Adam Rafferty, my assistant."

She extends a limp hand. "Pleased to meet you. Come in." She opens the door wider and then stands back to let us enter. "I hope you'll find my Chauncy boy."

"We're certainly going to try. It's been my experience that the sooner you get looking the better your chances of recovery are. Can we check out the backyard? There might be something there that will point us to whoever took him." Mike follows the woman across the foyer and into a bright, spacious kitchen.

I'm right behind, looking for any chew toy or object the dog might have left an imprint on. The dog's bowl and water dish are in the corner, next to a set of French doors that open up to a large deck and yard.

Lisa is barely able to speak as she tells Mike about letting the dog out and her horror when she discovered he was missing. All the while she's talking I'm running my hand over a plush designer dog bed on the opposite end of the room. For a moment it's like I'm inside the dog, hungry for breakfast and fighting the urge to take a pee on the leg of the table. That's Chauncy's life. Once the biological needs are squared away, his joy lies in the touch of this woman's hand scratching his belly.

Outside, I'm in my own head, ignoring Mike and the woman. Instead, I'm following Chauncy's usual pattern. He marks the two fruit trees before going to the corner of the yard to take care of the rest of it. But before he's there, two men come through a gate in the fence, coming toward him. One guy is tall, skinny and bald but the other one, the one with the raw steak in his hands, is burly with gray hair. The hackles go up on Chauncy's back, and his throat rumbles in a growl that I can feel in my windpipe. These guys are strangers invading his space. But that steak... *I'm* even salivating, licking my lips like Chauncy.

"What are you doing?" Lisa has been watching me, and now she's curious, coming over to me.

I place my hand on her arm, and her life, specifically the nightmare divorce she's going through, hits me like a hammer. The soon-to-be ex has vowed to destroy her after catching her out in an affair. Funny thing, though; she's only concerned with the missing dog. There wasn't a lot of love for the husband at any point in the marriage.

Mike answers her question. "Adam has psychic abilities, Lisa. I won't lie to you. Finding a missing person is hard but a missing pet? Is there anyone who may have taken Chauncy to get back at you?"

I pipe up before she has a chance. "Your ex. He didn't take the dog but he hired people to do it. They lured Chauncy with a T-bone."

Her eyes go wide staring at me. "What? You know...?" She recovers from the shock of my perception pretty quickly, her face contorting in anger. "You think *Tom* did this? That little weasel. I'll kill him if he hurts Chauncy! Tom never liked him. Chauncy was always *my* dog."

She sidles closer, clinging to me. "Find him. Please, I'll do anything to get him back." Her fingers begin to knead the flesh of my forearm.

I nod, extricating my arm and edging closer to Mike. This is crazy, but I'd swear there's more she's offering here than just Mike's fee. And it isn't all about the dog. Her gaze lingers as she's taking in my ripped jeans and back up to lock eyes with me. Her tongue darts out and touches her lower lip so quickly I almost miss it.

Oh my God. This woman, almost old enough to be my mother is *attracted* to me? No. No. And triple no. Not gonna happen.

Mike senses the oddness that infuses the situation like a bad smell. He speaks quickly, "We'll do what we can, Lisa. But we have to go now. Give me the contact info for your husband. I'll cover that base while Adam does his thing."

When Lisa is busy with Mike, giving him the address and phone number, I wander to the wooden gate. Her house is the last one on the block, and there's a side street next to her backyard. An image of a white cargo van peeling away flashes in my mind's eye. But all I could make out of the plate was that it was a New York license starting with the letters DCC or DOC.

I manage to evade Lisa's outstretched hand and race back to the house. There's a tennis ball missing half the bright yellow shell on Chauncy's bed. I slip it into my pocket and then hurry to the front door.

Mike looks puzzled when he gets into the car and starts the engine. He shoots a look at me, "Again you lit out of there like your ass was on fire. Granted she's old enough to be your mother but you were kind of rude, kid."

"Are you kidding? She cheated on him. That's why he's filed for divorce. I even picked up on the guy she was with. He's built like a quarterback with tree trunks for thighs. So why me? I'm not exactly Mr. Six-Pack Abs. I don't think it was my boyish charm either."

Even though his face is twisted in disbelief he ponders. "Maybe your luck's changing, kid. I mean you had a lock on that redhead last night. And now Lisa? Funny, I would have thought she'd be attracted to me. She wasn't bad-looking either." He wheels the car out of the drive and then clicks the radio on.

The tinny voice of a woman reciting the news blares through the speakers. "The woman found next to a dumpster in the Food City parking lot early this morning has been identified as Cynthia Brooks. Miss Brooks was an early childhood educator at Linklater School. Police are asking for any information from people who may have seen Miss Brooks in the last twenty-four hours. Miss Brooks had been brutally assaulted resulting in her death."

The air is suddenly sucked out of the car's interior. My heart pounds fast as I look over at Mike.

I point at the radio. "Mike… that was the redhead in the bar last night. Cynthia Brooks."

NINE

His jaw drops, and his eyes widen in a double take staring at me. He has to swerve quickly to avoid running into a parked car. "Shit, Adam! Are you sure? Maybe there're a few Cynthia Brooks in this town."

It's hard to get the words out when my mouth has dried up like a mud puddle on a hot day in July. "Yes! Cynthia worked as a teacher with small kids. There can't be two of them!" Oh my God! That poor, poor girl. What a waste of her life.

"You've got to go to the police station, Adam. Hell, I saw her last night as well. I'll need to make a statement too." Mike's face is tight glancing over at me. "You went home last night when you ran out of the bar, right?"

"Well, yeah!" This time it's my turn for the jaw drop. "You don't think I had anything to do with her death, do you?" But immediately following my outrage is remembering the crazy monkey sex with that specter. My gut sinks through the plush leather seat. That thing has something to do with what happened to Cynthia. It's too coincidental. It killed her. I don't know how I know this, but I do. I'd stake my life on that fact.

"Do you have anyone who can corroborate your story?"

His voice has taken on an officious edge which gets my back up even further.

"What the hell, Mike!"

"Look, I know you're innocent, okay? But the police are going to want a suspect, and you, my friend, will be a person of interest to them. Don't worry, I still have amigos on the force. I can maybe pull some strings."

"Will you listen to yourself? I'm innocent!" It pops into my head, Doug's knock on my door this morning. "Hey. My roommate heard me last night. He even commented on it this morning, so he can back me up."

"Whaddaya mean he '*heard* you'? What the hell were you doing?" Now he thinks I'm a total perv, from the look he shoots me.

I dry-scrub my face, buying time. Should I tell him everything? Either way he's gonna think I'm crazy. After taking a deep breath I turn to him. "Do you believe in demons, Mike?"

Again, his eyes flash almost as wide as his gaping mouth. "What? What are you talking about?"

We're back in the town center again, and the police station is just up on the next block. "Pull over. This is a long story that you need to hear. But believe me when I say it's true." This is gonna be tough. I can hardly believe it, and I experienced it!

From the look on his face, he thinks I've lost it, but he stops the car to hear me out.

Turning slightly to face him. "Okay, let's try another angle. Do you believe in God, heaven, and angels? The Bible?"

"Yeah, for the most part. I was raised Episcopalian and—"

"If there's a God representing good then it stands to reason that there's a polar opposite, representing evil. It's that whole thing about balance in the universe."

"Wait a minute. You're telling me you can see these things too... angels and demons?" From the way he's gripping the steering wheel, white knuckled, it's a toss-up as to whether he's fascinated or horrified.

"Not usually. Of course I see spirits all the time. Not

everyone who dies is ready to cross over to the next realm. People who die suddenly or who love another person so much that they don't want to leave them... I see them."

I take another deep breath and keep going, "As for angels, I've seen people who glow with silver auras. I believe they're either angels, or people who are so highly evolved that they're the next best thing. The Dalai Lama is definitely one."

"And people like Ted Bundy, Charles Manson... you think they're demons? Is that what you're saying?"

"I'm not sure. I've never met either of those guys. For sure, they're psychopaths. Maybe there's a demonic influence going on with people who commit horrible atrocities. But to get back to my point..." I swallow hard and continue, "I saw a demon yesterday. It's the same one I saw when I was twelve."

He's silent now, waiting for the connection to Cynthia.

"When you see a demon, Mike, you don't forget it. Believe me. They're dark and very foul. I almost threw up when it touched me." Even now as I tell Mike about this my gut rolls and the scratches it put on me, burn. "It's become attached to me somehow. It's in my head sometimes, saying things."

"What kinds of things? Like to kill someone or something?" He edges closer to the door.

I shake my head. "Nothing that overt... yet. It kind of taunts and goads me. And that girl, Cynthia, at the bar—"

"So, you're possessed?" His voice on that last word had come out kind of squeeky, so he clears his throat before continuing, "Just so ya know, this isn't helping your case regarding that poor girl's death."

He doesn't have to remind me how bad this looks. I can't tell the police all this supernatural shit, but for some reason I need Mike to understand it. I shake my head and continue.

"Not possessed exactly. But it was with me last night in the bar. It was a voice in my head, coaching me on what to say to her. Total bullshit lies, playing on her kindness and it was actually working!"

"Yeah...?"

"It was that thing! That demon. I even saw it when I went

to the bathroom. There was a darkness surrounding me that I've never seen before. That's why I bolted from the bar. I didn't want to take advantage of Cynthia. And believe me, that horrible thing wanted me to, desperately."

I tug the bottom of my T-shirt up to my chin. "It made these marks on me last night when I went home." My face warms up, but I have to come clean about everything. "I think it also molested me during the night. It got pretty wild. My roommate heard the commotion. He commented on the noise coming from my room."

He rolls his eyes and there's disgust in his curled lip. But it's better that he knows. I continue on, "I don't know how, but that bastard is responsible for Cynthia's murder. If it could cut me like this, what did it do to her? It hates the fact that I resisted doing what it wanted me to do with her. So it killed her to get back at me. I know it did."

He blinks hard a few times. "You're saying Cynthia's murderer is a demon?" Shaking his head, he continues, "That's not gonna go down well with the cops, Adam. You'll be lucky if they don't lock you up or put you in an insane asylum."

Funny thing is, even though he's shocked, I know he believes me. And getting this off my chest feels right. Aside from Amy, Mike is probably the only friend I've got who is able to hear this and not think I'm doing cheap drugs.

He turns to me, and there's a fiery determination in his stare. "Call me crazy, but I believe you. I read people pretty good so I know you're not lying. But you can't tell the police about this demon thing. For God's sake, leave that part out. You have a witness who'll attest to you being in your room all night. So that will clear you."

He turns the key in the ignition, "Now let's make our statement to the police and then find Lisa's dog."

TEN

I'm only a little late when I arrive at my delivery job. Phil tries to score points with his Aunt Hilda, making it more of a big deal than it is. After hearing about Cynthia's death, making a police statement as to my whereabouts last night, doing some sort of horizontal mambo with a demon and getting scratched in the process, I think I'm pretty well qualified to know what constitutes a *big deal.*

"Are you all right, Adam? You look pretty pale." Hilda ignores her nephew coming out from behind the counter to examine me.

"I'm fine. I had a rough night last night. I was awake most of the night after eating some bad food before bed." I smile when I see the concern on her face ease. I might as well go for consistency with the story I told Doug this morning. I think even the police detective—a friend of Mike's, which helped my case—bought it too.

"It's kind of a light day so far." She plucks the order sheets from the counter and hands them to me.

Phil looks up from his cell phone long enough to throw what he considers a zinger. "Just don't take advantage of that and be running the roads on our dime, Adam. Oh yeah, and thanks for that delivery in the boonies. I almost got a hernia lifting that statue into the van. Nice to know we can count on you—NOT!"

"I hope those porn sites you're always plugging into don't charge by the minute. Hilda might have to mortgage the business to pay the internet bill." I grab the keys from the counter and head out. But not before I notice the look of shock on Hilda's face become a glaring world of trouble for Phil. Looks good on him.

The first assignment, picking up three orders of flowers to go to the funeral home puts me on the east end of town. After dropping off the flowers I sit in the parking lot and take the dog's tennis ball from my pocket.

I close my eyes. I'm instantly transported into the dognappers vehicle. The drone of the van's wheels on blacktop, cars and transports whipping by comes through in my mind. The husband, who's behind this caper would want to get the dog as far away as possible.

I grip the ball tighter and really focus all my energy into Chauncy. Where *are* you, dog? If you can sit up and see the countryside, maybe there will be some kind of sign or marking to let me know where you are. I see fields flitting by in a flash, and a four-lane highway separated by a wide median. But this could be anywhere.

Wait! The marker passes in a blur, too quick to see the number only the familiar logo. He's on I-81 heading south. One other sense comes through from Chauncy. He's gotta pee, bad. He's even whining a little.

The gray-haired guy turns and fixes beady eyes on the dog before he says something to the man driving. Maybe... just maybe.

I'm putting every cell in my body to work on this. The van's turn signal is flashing and it's pulling off the main route. Yes! I see the sign announcing the small town of Pulaski. I grab my phone from my pocket and punch the numbers to reach Mike. He answers on the second ring.

"Mike. The dog's in a white van with New York plates. First letters DDC or DOC. They just pulled off the I-81 in Pulaski. Do you know any cops in that town?"

"On it." A click follows.

For the first time that day a sense of relief and happiness floods through me. It might only be finding a dog but at least it's something positive.

That feeling is short-lived, when I get the phone call from Mike later that night.

ELEVEN

It's about eight o'clock when I get home to find my roommate perched in his usual spot in front of the TV. He gets up and comes over, his face more sour looking than I've ever seen it before.

"The police questioned me about you. They wanted me to verify that you were in your room all last night, Adam." The hands on his hips are splayed while he rocks back and forth on the balls of his feet.

"Yeah. Well you told them I was, right?" I brush by him to get a soft drink from the fridge.

He follows right on my heels. "That's just it. When I thought about all the banging on the walls, the headboard of the bed thumping like a jackhammer, it hit me that maybe you weren't alone in there. And then I hear about this woman who was butchered last night."

His eyes are narrow, sizing me up. He's been waiting for me to see how I'll react when he springs this. "I told them about that, how all the noise woke me up. But I couldn't say that you were here all night. Maybe you brought her to your room and then went out again after, taking her home. Was she here last night, Adam?"

"No! I met her in the bar. I only had a drink with her, but I came home alone. I wasn't feeling well. I must have fallen asleep and was thrashing from the bad cramps in my gut. Hell, I can't say what I did in my sleep. I was in my bed last night, Doug. Sleeping and getting up to go to the bathroom. *Alone.*"

Great. He's put me squarely in the cops' crosshairs. I take a swig of the soda eyeing him over the rim of the can. I thought he'd back me up, but instead he's muddied the waters even worse. "I didn't kill that girl. I hope they catch whoever did."

He's still not buying it. Skepticism clouds his body in a red haze. And maybe there's a bit of jealousy mixed in as well. He's got no life but he thinks I do? Little does he know. I go by him on my way to the bedroom to lie down for a bit before I go out. Actually I might take a break from going to the bar after what happened last night.

Just as I'm settling onto the bed, my phone buzzes. Mike's name comes up on the screen. "Hey Mike. Did you get the dog?"

"I'm outside your building, Adam. You need to come down. I've got to talk to you."

My body slumps lower into the nest of pillows. What now? I know it can't be good. But the dog is safe. That much came through when he spoke. "I'll be right down."

I finish my soda and then my feet fly down the two sets of stairs. The Caddie is parked near the door, and he's sitting in the driver's seat while the dog looks out at me from the backseat. I slip into the car and reach back to give the dog a rub behind his ear.

"What's up?" When I turn to Mike my world tilts off its axis from the images flooding his head. Lisa's body, the blood smears on the wall showing her struggles to fight back even as she's being ripped open. Oh my God!

"Lisa's dead, Adam. When I went out to her place to drop the dog off, the front door was wide open. I went in and found her in the kitchen. I've seen some mangled bodies but what was done to this woman…" Mike is white as a ghost as he tells me this.

I try to clear the horrifying images that flood from his head to mine. The soft drink curdles in my gut, threatening to explode from my throat. There's even a coppery scent in my nose from all the blood on the floor and walls.

"I called the police and waited there until they came. I've made two statements regarding murdered women in *one day*, Adam. Hell, they may suspect *me* in all this." Mike swallows hard. "My God, it was terrible what was done to that poor woman. It could have happened only a couple hours before I found her. Rigor mortis hadn't even set in."

All the while he's talking, the feeling that this death and Cynthia's are connected grows like a cancer. Both women were attracted to me and now they're dead. I didn't kill them, but I've got a pretty good idea who did. That voice in my head has been silent since this morning, but I feel its presence.

Why is this happening? What the hell does this thing want?

After a few moments, Mike continues, "The police are looking closely at the ex-husband. Especially after he hired those knuckleheads to snatch the dog. When the police brought them in, Chauncy's microchip proved who the rightful owner is. Or rather was."

"But you don't believe that, do you? Stealing a dog is a wimpy-ass thing to do. That's a far cry from cold-blooded murder." I'm only echoing what I know he's thinking. The real answer is a presence between us that neither one of us wants to acknowledge.

"No. He's a schmuck, not a killer." Mike turns when Chauncy puts his paw on the back of the seat. He pets the dog's head a few times.

"You didn't tell the police about me working with you on this case." I know he hasn't but it would be good to hear it from him.

"Kid, if I did that they'd probably arrest you. Probably the only thing that stopped them from looking twice at me is the fact I'm one of them. They *know* me. But you... they'd be all over you like white on rice." He shakes his head.

"They questioned my roommate."

"I figured they would. Did he back you up?"

"Yeah, sort of. But he also hinted that I had someone in my room last night and that he couldn't vouch for my being there the whole time. What a jerk." I look back at the dog. His tongue lolls out over loose jowls as he sits panting softly, oblivious to his owner's fate. "What are you gonna do with Chauncy?"

Mike snorts. "I guess, I'll keep him until someone in Lisa's family comes to claim him. Hopefully she had a will and he's mentioned in it. No way is that ex-husband getting Chauncy."

The dog perks up at the mention of his name and nuzzles Mike's shoulder, leaving a large drool on his jacket. In a way, the two of them kind of resemble each other with the jowls and wrinkles.

"I'd better get going. I've got to hit the grocery store to get him something to eat." He pushes the dog back and then turns to start the car.

"Hang on." I fish my phone from my pocket and then snap a pic of the dog. A feeling of sadness washes through me when I think of sending this to my sister. It's maybe the first time I regret leaving my family. If I hadn't come to this town, maybe those two women would be alive.

TWELVE

As Mike drives away I stand outside the building deliberating on whether to go to the bar. God knows after hearing about Lisa, I could use a drink. But instead I go back in the building and trudge up the stairs. I need to keep a clear head to figure all of this out, especially with the police nosing around.

I stop short with my hand on the doorknob before going into the apartment. Something is wrong, terribly wrong. My heart skips a beat while a bead of sweat rolls down my spine. I'm afraid to go in there. Whatever waits inside is going to finish me for once and for all. The demon is so close to me now that I can smell its rotten stench.

The handle in my hand twists and the door creaks open all by itself. The air is heavy when I step inside. All of the lights are off but even so I know that I'm not alone. The mayhem that played out five minutes ago lingers in a room that is now freezing cold.

Doug is the latest victim. Even before I flick the lights on, a picture of his broken body flashes in my head. I feel his terror, see the glint on the stainless steel of the knife as it rises above him. A blinding hot pain rips through my chest and I stand frozen with fear. This was Doug's final moment.

He's splayed out on the kitchen floor next to the stove. Blood seeps from the multiple wounds in his chest coating his flannel shirt. The knife lays next to him, still dripping with his blood. Oh my God.

The sight of the blood and gore is horrifying and I back away slowly. Even so I almost slip in the pool of blood, barely grasping the frame of the doorway to keep from falling.

It's happened again! That demon did this, but why? People around me are being butchered. Who's next? Mike? My gut tightens. Amy? Oh no, not Amy!

Why hasn't it come after me? I've obviously pissed it off enough that it's on some kind of psycho killing spree. Seeing Doug's body sliced in a pool of blood brings home what Cynthia and Lisa faced. They didn't have a chance.

Oh my God! Poor guy. Doug wasn't a bad fella. He was quiet, going through a rough time after his divorce, but he never nagged me when I was a day short in covering my part of the rent. We weren't best buddies but still... He didn't deserve this. His only fault was knowing *me*.

"What do you want from me? Why are you doing this?" My screams reverberate in the still apartment. It's faint at first or maybe because my racing pulse pounds in my ears that I almost miss it entirely. But there's a chilling cackle and then silence.

Tears run down my face as I run to my room. I'm totally done for. It might just as well be me lying on that kitchen floor instead of Doug. This evil entity is surrounding me with death! Who would ever believe I didn't have anything to do with it? No one. I think even Mike would be hard-pressed to believe me now.

I grab my duffel bag from the closet and shove my clothes inside. I've got to get out of here before anyone else gets killed. Somewhere far, far away. Somewhere I can drop under the radar to avoid being picked up by the police. I'll rot in a jail cell for the rest of my miserable life if they find me. Somewhere that I'll be alone, not putting people in this demon's sights.

I'm in a daze running from the apartment out of the building. This is a nightmare, and there's no waking up from it!

The bus station! I'll catch the first bus out of here but... money. There's only sixty-eight dollars in my bank account. I have to use cash, leave no trace of where I'm going. The bank is only a block or two out of my way, but I have no choice even though I'm desperate to get off the street and away.

I gulp air and have to slow to a fast walk to catch my breath. It makes me wish I went to the gym on a regular basis, like Phil. Oh my God! I'm so scared I'm not even thinking straight. Got to get control before I screw up.

A police cruiser with the lights flashing approaches from down the street, and my heart almost stops. But they pass by, sirens wailing, racing to some accident or crime. But it won't be my apartment. Doug's body probably won't be found until someone misses him at work. Or maybe Hilda will miss me and send Phil over. Shit.

No. It's probably going to be Mike who checks it out and finds Doug.

I wish I could talk to Mike. Get his advice but it's too risky. He might become the next victim. He'd probably try to talk me out of running away too, but that's not an option. Not with Doug being murdered as well.

Darting over to the main street where my bank is, I clean out my account. Well, sixty dollars since it only spits out twenties. That ought to get me far enough away by bus.

In another twenty minutes, I pause long enough to take a few calming breaths and then go into the bus station. The arrival and departure schedule displayed on a large monitor above the ticket counter shows a bus leaving in ten minutes to the Big Apple and another going to Saranac Lake in fifteen. The sooner I get out of town the better, so New York City it is. Plus I could really disappear in New York.

When I walk over to the ticket counter, the old man behind it casts a world-weary glance at me, "Where to?"

My heart is still pounding hard from the run and it's

difficult to get the words out. "New York City. How much is the fare?"

The man eyes me with suspicion, the thought that I'm some kind of criminal or terrorist resonates in his mind. "Fifty-two dollars. I need to see some ID first."

I scoop my wallet out and plop my driver's license on the counter, trying all the while to keep my hand from shaking.

The old guy peers down at my license and then clicks a keyboard. His head rises as he stares at the computer screen. "Sorry. The last seat just sold from an online purchase."

It's never easy. "Fine. Saranac Lake will do."

He pushes my driver's license back to me. "That's in the opposite direction from New York City. You know that, right?"

"Yeah. I've got family in both places. Either one's good. I mean, I'll go to New York City after my visit in Saranac." Shit. I'm babbling, making me look even more flaky. And there's no way I want this guy to remember me. At. All.

"That'll be thirty-three fifty."

Well, that's one good thing. At least it leaves me with a little cash. God knows how long that will last, though. But first things first. Get out of town. I hand him the money and then take the ticket. A mechanical voice announces that the bus to Lake Placid and Saranac Lake is boarding at gate three.

I finish at the counter and drop my cell phone into a garbage bin on my way by. If the police track it down they'll find it in a landfill far from where I'm going to be.

Tears sting the backs of my eyes. This evil entity has wreaked death and destruction of innocent people. Why? Why Cynthia, Lisa, and even stranger, why Doug? If I knew the answer I might have a chance of stopping it. Instead I'm fleeing like a fugitive, and I'll probably never see my family ever again.

This demon is happy doing this to me. It may not be speaking in my head, but I know it's watching, lurking just out of reach, hidden from my perception. So help me God, I'd give anything to kill this thing! I've never known rage before this asshole decided to screw up my life.

The attendant at the bus takes my ticket and I climb the steps into the bus. I spy a couple of empty seats halfway back and make my way there. I slip into the one at the window, and put my bag on the seat next to me. With any luck there won't be stops along the way picking up more passengers. There's no way I want to talk to anyone right now. Besides which my best chance of surviving this nightmare is becoming a nonperson, someone people don't even notice.

***

For the next couple hours it's a running replay of every interaction I've had with this demon from when I was twelve right up to hearing its evil cackle in the apartment earlier. It said it wants to use me to experience life. A night with Cynthia looked promising with all its coaching but I derailed that pretty fast. So it killed her for revenge on me. And it made sure I knew it. Why else would it visit me during the night and mark me with scratches? The thing had probably killed her by that time.

And if it wanted me to take advantage of Lisa, I'd sidestepped it once again. Surely, this isn't just about this spirit or whatever wanting to experience sex through me. But it had said that it waited for me since I was twelve. Waited till I was a young man obsessed—like most guys—with getting laid. Turns out I wasn't as weak and able to be manipulated as it had thought. So it got angry. Actually enraged is more accurate. Enough to slaughter two women.

But Doug? Doug doesn't fit this theory. Why did it kill him?

It's enough to make my head explode trying to figure this thing out. I stare out at the night sky, no closer to figuring out what this thing is up to than before.

Another curious aspect is how silent this demon has become. No more conversation. The last time it was in my head, it goaded me about my father having the perfect son, Seth, and of course the perfect daughter, Amy. Pretty weak stuff considering I'd lived my life already accepting that I was a disappointment to my folks. What was the point of it doing that?

Lights in the distance signal that my destination isn't that far away. To confirm it, the driver's voice fills the coach giving passengers departing at Saranac Lake a ten-minute warning. It's only when my ears pop that I realize that since we left Watertown the bus has been steadily climbing the landscape, making its way to the Adirondack Mountains.

The bus slows, and I notice the road sign announcing that we're entering the town of Saranac Lake, population 5,528. That's even smaller than where I left. Maybe I should have waited for another bus going to New York City, to become lost in a sea of people. But nothing is forever. I'll get some mindless job to get enough money to leave as soon as possible.

It's after midnight when I hoist my bag over my shoulder and leave the bus. There's only one other passenger, a middle-aged woman who is met by what looks to be her husband. Walking along the sidewalk beside stores and buildings no higher than three stories, it has the feel of a place that's been frozen in time. It appears like little has changed from when it was built.

A tall church spire a block away and off the main drag catches my eye. Even if I am lucky enough to find a cheap motel, I'd still come up short in cash. Considering the demon that's probably somehow hitchhiked along with me, spending the night on church property isn't the worst idea I've ever had.

THIRTEEN

I walk along the shores of a lake, enjoying the warm summer day. Seagulls squawk and swoop down to the water to catch their lunch from the sparkling waves. I become aware of a girl walking about ten feet in front of me. Long, honey-blond hair streams over her bare shoulders, cascading down to the top of a pink sundress. Her bare feet are soundless when she jumps from stone to stone on an outcrop lining the shore, but her laugh at each smooth landing rings in the air. She knows I'm following, trying to catch up but just as I start to close the gap, she darts ahead.

I need to talk to her. There's no romance or wish to sleep with her. Just talk. That's all. I don't know why, but the need keeps growing until I have to call out.

When she turns, her eyes capture me immediately. They're the color of the sky before a storm, deep-gray and flecked with the last traces of pure blue. There's an innocent quality in the smile that starts to form but doesn't quite finish before her gaze flickers to something behind me. Her eyes fly open in terror before she turns and races up through the field that borders the lake.

I look over my shoulder to see what spooked her just when it looked like I'd get to meet her. It's darkness, a shadow figure that follows my every step. A rumbling noise from its throat becomes louder and louder...

My eyes fly open at the throbbing drone in the air. Chilling dampness seeps through my body and a wall of gray rock hulks close to my face. I jerk, bolting up and looking around at the green lawn and street next to it.

It comes to me gradually. The church. I'm in a strange town with not even twenty dollars to my name, sleeping outdoors.

It seems like I only just fell asleep, lost in a dream of some girl at a lake. Even though I'm tired, there's no way I can stay here much longer. The drone that woke me is actually a lawnmower pushed by an elderly man on the patch of grass next to the church's front step. I shove the sweatshirt I used as a blanket back into my makeshift pillow—the duffel bag—and creak up to my feet. My body aches in places I never knew I had from laying on the cold ground.

After finger-combing my hair to some sort of order, I shoulder the strap of the bag and make for the street. The sun peeks through the leaves of stately oak trees, and from the angle of the light, it's probably around eight in the morning. The air is so clear and fresh, and the day already so warm that it makes all that happened yesterday surreal. It's like it happened to another person.

And that dream had been so peaceful. Up until that part with the shadow behind me, plunging me back down to earth with a thud. Even in my dreams I'm not free of it.

Pushing the door open of a small mom-and-pop diner, the aroma of coffee brewing, and bacon and toast is sweet torture. I take a booth next to the plate-glass window for a better view down the rest of the main street.

"Morning. Would you like a coffee to start?" It's already a foregone conclusion as the middle-aged woman sets the mug down and hands me a menu.

"Yes. Please. I don't need a menu. I'll have bacon, eggs over easy and whole wheat toast." I hold the mug up for her to pour me a cup. The woman has been doing this job for eons, never missing a beat as she pours and scoops the menu up again.

"You new in town or just visiting?" Her smile is genuine and really welcoming, a ray of sunshine that makes me feel better about coming to this place.

"I'm new. I just got in last night. Know any place that's hiring extra help? I'll take pretty much anything. Delivery, dishwasher, cleaner." But from the way her smile falters, she's coming up blank.

"Sorry. Tourist season heats up next month. There'll be lots of openings then." She starts to walk away but pauses. "Leave your name and number, and if I hear of anything I'll call you."

Not having a cell phone is going to be difficult. "That's okay. Just thought I'd ask." I drain the cup and then head to the bathroom.

As I'm washing my hands at the sink I glance into the mirror and my gut drops. It's back. That same darkness I saw in the bar that night is here surrounding me again. And what makes it worse is that I saw it in the dream of the girl walking next to the lake. A strange sensation quivers through my body.

That dream of the girl next to the lake is a premonition. She's here in Saranac Lake and so is the demon.

I was meant to come here.

The pieces of this nightmare puzzle fall into place. Doug was the one who didn't fit when I tried to figure this out last night. But with his death I have to leave Watertown. It is no coincidence that I am unable to get the bus to New York City. It was never part of the plan.

This thought does nothing to give me any peace of mind.

***

When I finish my breakfast in the diner I spy a Goodwill store across the street halfway down the block. If I have to sleep on the grounds of the church I might as well get something waterproof to put between me and the earth. It may be days before I'm able to get enough cash to afford a roof over my head.

And if I can't find work, there's always panhandling.

Wouldn't Mom and Dad be proud?

But there's no way I'm leaving this town. This predicament with that entity has to stop. It wants me here, so *here* is where I'll fight it off or die trying. One thing I know for sure. The killing of innocent people has got to stop. And if it takes staying here to accomplish that, I'll do it.

I cross the street to go into the Goodwill store, but a rare sight brings me to an abrupt halt. A silver aura surrounds the old lady who comes out of the store. I've only ever seen one other person with that kind of pure energy.

The old woman has the identical aura as my nana. I don't even need to do my sidey-eyes to see it, it's so powerful.

She spots me, and her dark eyes grow wide in fear. She steps back, letting the shopping bag fall to the sidewalk. She speaks in a low voice while raising her hands, her forefinger and pinky pointing at me to ward off evil.

She sees it! She knows all about this abomination shadowing me! Of course. This woman is highly gifted in the psychic realm. She practically glows with it. She can help me. And I desperately need help fighting this thing.

"Please. I need your help. You can actually *see* it." I take a step toward her but she rushes down the street, faster than I would have thought, given her age.

She looks over her shoulder and pulls the dark sweater tighter to her throat. "No! Leave me alone." Grabbing the handle of a rusty, gray car, she almost falls over herself getting in. The car roars to life and lurches out onto the street.

I watch her drive away until she disappears around a corner. The fear on her face, and her actions tell me that this thing is even more dangerous than I thought. If it scared the hell out of *her*, what chance do I have?

I pick up the bag that she abandoned. The imprint she's left is strong and I see her house, little more than a cottage really, in the country. There's a lake not far from it.

This woman can help me. Maybe she's the only one who can. I start walking in the direction she went. I've got to reach her.

FOURTEEN

She can't stop me. Although it will be fun seeing her die trying.'

My back stiffens at the insidious voice in my head. It's been silent for so long that it's jarring hearing its whispered words. I continue walking steadily down the road, ignoring the thundering beat of my heart. The fact that it's only now chosen to speak confirms that I've made the right decision.

Squaring my shoulders back, I even manage to sound calm. "You can't overpower her. Unlike the other innocent people you slaughtered, the old lady recognized you. She knows about you and that makes you nervous." Saying the words out loud strengthens my conviction. I sense the thing squirming, becoming more agitated.

'I've met her kind before. Trust me. It never worked out well for them. Her blood will be on your hands, Adam. Do you really want more death?'

"Just my own if that's what it takes to be rid of you." At the sound of a vehicle coming down the road behind me I turn to face it. A black truck, the first vehicle that's come down this road in almost an hour barrels down the road, kicking up a rooster tail of dust. I go to the side of the road watching it close the gap between us.

"You waited a long time for someone as gifted as me. And then waited till I was old enough for you to fully exploit. Do you really want to threaten any more people when all it would take is stepping in front of this truck? I'll finish this for once and for all!"

Detached peace fills my mind. Which surprises me on another level as I watch the truck getting closer and closer.

In a few more seconds I could be dead! But the nightmare my life has become would be over. I wouldn't be responsible for any other person dying. I couldn't live with myself if that happened again.

I watch it get closer, the roar of the engine filling my ears. Just one step onto the road and...

'Fine! I won't kill anyone!' The rage in its bellow sends a shooting pain through my head.

A couple seconds later the truck whizzes by making my hair swoosh up. The young man behind the wheel doesn't even look at me as he passes, totally clueless how close he was to becoming involved in my death. I'm glad for his sake that he wasn't.

My eyes close and my legs almost give out from under me. Now that the adrenaline spike in my body has evaporated my legs turn to rubber and I'm kind of giddy.

I tug the strap of my duffel bag higher and stagger a little walking down the country road. The mountain air has a clean freshness that I didn't notice before. The grass and trees look greener. The sky, mottled with wispy clouds, seems closer. Even though my knees are kind of wobbly, I'm aware of my heartbeat, the blood coursing through my veins and... What the hell? There's a little tingle and fullness in my groin now that the danger to my body has passed.

And there's blessed silence in my mind. No doubt the thing is sulking like a spoiled child. But it worked. It knew I would have done it, kill myself, and it wants me alive. Good to know.

The road disappears behind a bend in the road. For all the pretty countryside with the lake nearby, there aren't that many houses out this way. I only passed one in the last hour of walking. When I round the curve I see it. The old lady's house with the gray car parked in the driveway. The clapboard house is only one story with a veranda out front that runs the length of it. There's a shed outbuilding, to the side, and her whole front yard is transformed into neat rows of sprouting vegetables.

I turn in and walk up the dirt drive, past the old car. As I'm about to step up onto the bottom stair of her veranda, it's like my foot hits an invisible wall. I'm barely able to keep my balance, arms windmilling to the sides.

The door opens, and the old lady stands there. Her eyes narrow. "I told you to stay away from me." Again she is doing that thing with her fingers. Even though she's doing it to ward off the evil that clings to me, I've seen rock stars make that same gesture to 'rock on'.

I chuckle at the weird random thoughts popping into my head. Maybe I really am losing it. Shit, I just about committed suicide, didn't I?

I take a deep breath before I speak. "I'm in trouble, lady. I know you can see this thing, this evil entity that's attached itself to me. But I'm innocent. I didn't *ask* for this." The last few words are a mere whisper. From the hard defensive look in her gaze this isn't working. I fight the tears stinging the back of my eyes. If she doesn't help me, I'm done for.

She steps closer but her hand never lowers. Her eyes are mere slits examining not only my sad state of dress but the darkness that is inside me. "Adam. The first man. He had trouble with a demon too."

"Yeah. I'm Adam Rafferty, Mrs. Kovacs. But as for that biblical story and my name, just coincidence, I guess." She's not the only one who can pick up information just by a look.

"There is no such thing as coincidence, boy. And this thing... this evil spirit is strong. I'm old. I've seen it before and I can't help you. I'm sorry." She backs away, never dropping her gaze. Her hand clutches the side of the door as she takes another step to go back inside.

"No! You *have* to help me! You know how to banish it." I lurch forward but it's like hitting a wall that bounces me back onto my ass on her walkway. I look up at her framed in the doorway, her aura of silver light now contains threads of purple. Hope rises in my chest at that trace of compassion evident in her color now.

"You keep your distance." She's still standing there watching me closely. A sly smile forms on her wizened lips. "You don't have much choice in that. I've made sure of it. You will not enter my home."

It's then that I notice the barrier that's been keeping me at bay. It's a wavering shimmer that extends from the bottom step of her house to the roof. It's what forced me back, powerful enough that I landed on my ass. "How did you do that? Teach me. If you can do this, prevent this thing inside me from entering your home, you can *help* me. I'm innocent. I just want this gone!"

"It isn't that simple, Adam. You know what this thing is capable of. The blood of three innocent people cry out to me, yet I can't risk helping them, let alone you." She starts to close the door, looking down at her feet.

I was wrong about her. What I saw as compassion was only relief that her defenses were holding.

Tears fall down my cheeks as the door closes and she's gone. "I'm not leaving! I don't have anywhere else to go. You said you've seen this thing before. What is it? What does it want from me?" But silence and a closed door are the only answer.

I sink to my knees, totally racked with despair and sorrow—for Cynthia, for Lisa, and for Doug. And also for myself. My last hope of getting rid of this thing just closed the door on me. Tears and snot fall onto the old lady's muddy walkway.

'Told ya. I'm more powerful than that old bat. At least she's smart enough to realize it.'

I slump down even lower. If the earth would open and swallow me up, it might be a blessing. "What do you want from me? I'll do anything. No killing, but whatever it takes if you'll just leave me alone. I can't take much more of this."

The chuckle that oozes from its maw sends a shiver down my spine. What am I agreeing to? I feel like I've sold my soul to the devil. A wicked she-beast that marked me for her own when I was twelve.

***

The sun is low in the sky by the time I pull myself up. The long walk out here carrying this burden of guilt and horror has left me weak. I wander over to the garden and pluck some snow peas from the vine. A glance at the house shows no sign of life. I may not be able to cross her threshold but neither can she hide in there forever. I know she's in the shadows of the house watching me.

I strip the vines of all the fleshy peas, the only thing that's ripe, and then make a show of eating them. I don't even *like* peas, but it's been a long time since breakfast at the diner. I stare right back at the old lady. There. Take that. I've robbed you of all your precious peas. And I know just by touching the leaves and stems that she's put not only back-breaking work into this garden but there's a little of her soul here as well. This garden sustains and nourishes her in return for her loving care.

'That's the spirit, Adam. That'll hurt the old bat, right in the bread basket. There's hope for you yet.'

"SHUT UP!" The echo reverberates through the air, and I know the vein in my forehead bulges just like my mom's when she's pissed. Thinking of my family fills me with more rage. I'm never going to see any of them again, and I have this '*thing*' to thank for that.

And it still hasn't let me in on its plans, what it wants from me. I'm like a marionette, and it's holding the strings unless that old lady will relent and help me.

I wander across her yard to the back where there's a shed, leaning a little to the side. Poking my head inside the smell of camphor and earth fill my nose. At least she didn't put that spell on this place and it's better than sleeping outside.

Especially being this far out in the country with woods bordering the property. God knows what kinds of animals live in there, maybe bears or wolves or something equally nasty.

I shove the wheelbarrow and garden tools to the side wall making a small space on the dirt floor for me to sleep. The light is beginning to fade and I'd better get that out of the way before it's completely black. There aren't any streetlights and her house is too far away to shed much light from the windows.

But if I'm back here, what's stopping her from running out to the car and hightailing it out of here? I finish emptying my knapsack and even the old lady's goodwill bag. There's just a sweater and a pair of rubber rain boots in it.

Then I leave the musty shed to take up my vigil on her walkway again. I'm not leaving and neither is she. The air has turned damp and chilly, and I pull the sides of my jean jacket tighter together. The smell of wood smoke catches my attention and I look up at her roof. A thin tendril of gray smoke floats up from her chimney.

She's inside nice and warm, probably filled with a hot meal while I sit out here with a belly full of peas rumbling around painfully in my bowels.

Nice.

I race to the edge of the woods, barely getting my pants down in time. It seems her fresh produce has had its revenge on me. Reduced to shitting in the woods like an animal.

FIFTEEN

When I emerge from the shed after a restless night from the bugs crawling over my neck and face, I can barely believe my eyes. On the mammoth tree stump behind the house is a muffin and a red thermos. The old lady, Mrs. Kovacs left this for me? Chocolate chips melt in my mouth when I take a bite, My fingers are still kind of numb as I remove the top of the thermos and wash the muffin down with hot tea. It's manna from heaven, fallen from a clear blue sky, the sun well above the horizon.

She comes out on her back step, hanging a wet dishrag on the line running to a tree at the rear of the property. She barely glances my way but her voice breaks the stillness. "Do you still want my help?"

My heart flips up in my chest as I look at her. "Yes. Please Mrs. Kovacs."

Her dark eyes skewer me when she turns. Gnarly fingers clutch the stone of a necklace hanging over a gaunt chest. "Margrit. Call me by my given name." Her chin jerks up, and she looks at the pile of thick chunks of wood heaped in a mound. "Know how to split wood? Cut those up into quarters and we'll talk. Do the whole pile." With that she turns and disappears into the house again.

'Screw her! Grab that ax and beat her door down. There's more food inside. Bacon, eggs, toast slathered with gobs of butter. She's holding out, giving you a measly muffin and tepid tea.'

For a moment my mouth waters at the image of a decent breakfast. My fingers curl around the ax, and I take a step toward her back step. The door is flimsy and maybe she doesn't have that witchy spell on it. She had a good night's sleep in a warm bed while I battled spiders and centipedes.

The door flies open and she stands there, once more doing that evil-eye thing with her fingers. "Fight it! The demon is clouding your judgment."

I stop short and the ax burns my hand so much that I yelp flinging it from me. The old lady's aura swirls, getting bigger and denser as she stares at me. But it's not me she's staring down. It's this 'thing'.

Shit. For a few moments it actually had me doing its bidding! I spit a gob of saliva onto the ground. That demon put the image of the warm food in my brain and I want nothing to do with it.

A shooting pain in my head threatens to blind me in its intensity. Oh my God. The foul sensation of rage runs through me—not mine but the entity's rage. With her help I beat the demon back and it's really pissed now.

"Good boy. Now split my wood." This time she actually smiles before she goes in the house.

I can't believe how much her praise affects me. The only time I felt this good about myself was with my grandmother. And it's the first time I've felt genuine hope that I can get rid of this... this paranormal leech.

But it's also scary how easily I succumbed to its words. I've got to be really careful. And listening to this woman is the key.

Another first. I have never followed anyone's advice. Even my grandmother's.

***

Hours later, I swipe a bead of sweat from my forehead and prop the ax against the tree stump. All of the wood is about a foot long, in four-inch sections, stacked in a neat wall close to her back step. My T-shirt clings to my chest, and my arms ache from splitting all the wood. I don't think I've ever felt this bone weary before but it's a good tiredness. And all the while I worked, that voice never spoke. There is a stillness in my mind that I guess is close to yoga or meditation.

The door opens, and the old lady appears carrying a tray. Ice clicks in the pitcher of water and there's a plate of sandwiches next to a glass. After setting it down on the wooden boards of the stoop she takes a step over to the rocking chair and sits. "Eat. I want to tell you a story."

I rush over and lift the jug of water not even bothering to fill the glass but gulping it right down. The coldest beer never tasted as good as that icy water. It's empty in a few seconds. "Thanks." I ease down onto the step. "Not just for the food and drink but for your help too."

She nods but there's no smile accompanying it. "Back in Italy, many years ago a young woman in my family was attacked by this demon. Sasha was psychically gifted even more so than you. She was also very beautiful, and as a result, the poor girl was pursued by many men. She could have had the pick of the whole town, but she never wanted to be tied to one man. And she definitely never wanted children."

"Italy? You don't sound Italian."

"I'm not. I'm 'Romi.' My family… we were gypsies. We wandered across the land, our own culture. We were in Italy when this occurred." She paused. "When that beast took Sasha…"

'She wasn't all that special. Sasha wasn't nearly as gifted as you. Don't believe this witch. She'll trick you and use you up. How do you think she became as strong as she is?'

The words are a hiss that almost make me choke on the bite of sandwich. It's not just the shock of hearing it again; it's the malignancy of the tone. A picture of a young woman, her dark hair flying up behind her as she races through a forest, her clothes torn and hanging in rags, fills my mind's eye. It isn't just the desperate image, but her terror fills me with dread.

"Stay focused, Adam. This is important." The old lady sits forward, and her eyes seem to spark while her hand clutches the stone at her chest.

"How can I focus when this thing keeps whispering at me? How do I get it to stop?" I push the plate of half-eaten sandwiches away when my stomach threatens to erupt up my throat. I can almost smell the stink of this hellish being, the rotting sewage of its core.

Again the aura that surrounds the old woman becomes denser and expands outward. She's fighting this thing, pulling on power sources from the earth and air around her. A sense of calm quiet infuses my mind and body with her effort.

I need to know how to do that!

I start to get up to get closer to her, to touch her and know but she stops me, once more giving me the hand signal. "Don't come any closer. Stay where you are."

I sink back down. She's still frightened of it. I can't push her too far or she will refuse to help me. Death and this demon still cling to me and she's right to be wary. With an exhausted sigh, I say, "Okay. Go on with your story."

She's silent for a few moments settling back into her chair and looking off into the distance. "Sasha was my cousin. I watched her go from being a free spirit to one who was hunted and eventually destroyed by this demon. It used a man's body when it assaulted her."

This time when she sits quietly her eyes well with tears and she's having trouble forming words. For once, I'm able to control my mouth and let her take her all the time she needs before I pepper her with questions.

"Sasha was banished by the elders when it became known she was pregnant. Honor is most important to Romi and she wasn't married. My grandmother pleaded Sasha's case. She knew that Sasha hadn't been with any man, that this was the work of an evil demon, but they didn't listen to her. There is nothing worse to a Romi than banishment. Sasha threw herself off a cliff rather than have that baby. She knew."

I wait a few moments out of respect but finally I blurt, "This thing I saw when I was twelve and then again a few days ago is a woman. It can't be the same one that drove your cousin to suicide."

Her chin juts out, and she practically spits the words, "And you threatened to kill yourself as well. I know that. It was a brave though foolish threat that worked for a while. This entity wants you alive, wants to use you to experience what it so desperately craves.

"What? What does it want with me? What does it crave that it would kill to get me in this town?"

"Life."

I snort. "Life. It said that it wants to experience things using me. When I threatened to kill myself by stepping in front of a truck, it actually agreed to what I wanted. So my plan wasn't all that foolish, Margrit. I made it promise not to hurt or kill anyone else."

This time it's she who guffaws. "And you believe it? You are dealing with the master of lies and treachery. It's found a gold mine in you, Adam, and it's not going to leave easily."

So here we were again talking about the problem, but no suggestion from her as to how to fix it. I slump lower onto the step. Even if it were fixed, there's a trail of bodies behind me. They'll blame me for the murders and lock me away for life.

Probably Mike has discovered Doug's body by now. No doubt the police have an arrest warrant drawn up for me. There's no going back even if the old lady can help me.

"Stop feeling sorry for yourself! Every time you do, this wraith gains more control over you. It's time to be a *man*, Adam. Have some self-respect and strength of character. And for starters taking a bath wouldn't hurt." She rises to her feet but makes no move to come any closer.

"How? You won't let me in the house. I have to go to the woods to relieve myself." I know she just gave me shit for pitying myself, but going to the forest to relieve myself, getting eaten alive by bugs in the process is more in an animal's repertoire.

"Stop it! I left a bar of soap and a towel on the front walkway. There's a lake on the other side of those woods. When you return, leave your dirty clothes on the step. I'll also expect you to weed my garden before you get any supper, unless you'd prefer more of my snow peas." This time she actually lets a smile crease her face.

The old coot! She knew she'd have the last laugh with the fresh snow peas. And she's getting a lot of work from me, splitting logs, and weeding her garden, all the while being all Yoda-like. "Sure you don't want me to paint your house while I'm at it?"

"That's tomorrow's work." She actually has the nerve to cackle.

"You really going to help me or what?"

"I already have. When you wanted to touch me and gain my power, it would have ended any chance of banishing this entity. This thing is sneaky. You thought that getting close to me was your own thought." She sniffed, her mouth turned down at the corners. "It wasn't."

There's no smile now. And her fingers clutch that stone on her chest even harder as she looks behind me. It reminds me of that dream I had at the church my first night in this town when the young woman saw the shadow man and fled. A shiver ripples across my shoulders. It was so powerful and sneaky that I didn't even know the urge in my head wasn't my own.

I don't know where I end and it begins…

Oh boy.

SIXTEEN

After grabbing the soap and towel I stop at the shed to get a change of clothes to take with me. The smell of camphor is gone, replaced with a stench of an open sewer. But that's not all. The old lady's sweater is in shreds, smeared with a dark substance that the smell leaves no question as to what it is. It's swarming with blue bottle flies. Her rubber boots are slashed hanging over the wooden handle of the rake and shovel.

The demon had been thoroughly pissed by the peace I enjoyed while splitting her wood. It took out its anger with the raging destruction of her stuff in the shed. So this is good, right? I try to convince myself that she must be a real threat to its plans. And the fact that she wasn't attacked means that it can't penetrate her spiritual armor.

Still. The wanton destruction and the stench make me queasy. I pluck the sweater and boots up and toss them as far as I can, throwing them to the side of the property. I grab my duffel bag and take clean clothes from it. Thankfully this demon thing didn't mess with my stuff.

As I pick a path through the dense woods each step feels

heavy. Or maybe it's knowing that I'm not alone, that this shadow demon is weighing me down. And it's deathly still in the stand of trees. Not a breath of wind or sound of life anywhere around. I'm not a great hiker but even I know that this isn't natural. There should be insects hovering or even birds chirping. It's as if all are holding their breaths so as not to be noticed by me or my psychic stalker.

Finally the tree growth thins and the blue of the lake can be seen. The shoreline is rocky, reminding me of the dream again. It's even more familiar when I notice the field about five hundred feet away bordering the shoreline. The air is clear and warm with seagulls making their presence known, squawking.

I peel the T-shirt off smelling the pungent sweat from my work earlier. It's such a pretty beach area that I'm reminded of a family holiday at Hamlin Beach, swimming with Amy. I pause for a moment checking the area for any life before peeling off my jeans and shoes. And just like at Hamlin, the water is freezing and rocks bite into the soles of my feet. It's a bittersweet memory, knowing I'll probably never see Amy again, or if I do, it'll be in the visitor's room at some penitentiary.

When I'm up to my thighs in icy water I take the plunge, submersing my body and head. The shock of the frigid water takes my breath away for a moment or two. The day may be warm and the sun blistering hot, but it's early in the season for swimming; this lake is probably filled with melting snow from the mountain runoff. Needless to say, I don't dally in soaping myself from head to toe and getting the hell out of there.

But when I get out, my step is surer, and the frigid water bath has helped clear my head. The old lady was right about doing this. I just hope she's also right about getting rid of that demon. God knows, the story of her cousin was depressing, killing herself when that demon thing raped her. Who knew that would even be possible? But considering it had killed three people and assaulted me it was capable of anything.

I look down to check the scratches it left on me. Aside from a slight itch, they've faded.

I gasp when it hits me. The story of Margrit's cousin and my own experience with this demon have one thing in common. There's a strong sexual element, but more than that, is the obscene thought that it wants to *procreate.* The grandmother knew it and so did Sasha. That's why she ended her life and this thing's offspring.

But why would this demon want anything to do with me? True, it had appeared to me as a woman but could it actually become pregnant? Not that there is any chance of me cooperating. Good luck with that one. I towel off and then slip the clean clothes on. This is something to talk to Margrit about. It may help in figuring out how to ditch this thing.

I make my way through the forest again and see the old lady digging in the side of the yard where I threw the sweater and boots. When she sees me her hand clutches the dark stone and she waves me off. Even though I just bathed, her actions remind me of the dirty entity that has infiltrated my body. I give her a wide berth walking by to take my old clothes to the front walkway.

"The paint and brushes are in the shed. If you notice a strange smell there, it's because I cleansed it with a sage smudge while you were gone. I also left a pillow and blanket for you." She goes back to the task of burying the sweater and boots which the demon destroyed.

When I enter the shed the air in there does smell better, lighter even. And she's tidied up the nest I curled up in, adding a canvas ground cover to keep the dampness out. A used brush rests on a large can of paint sitting next to the bed. I pick up the items along with a screwdriver and take them to the side of her house.

I'm stirring the paint when she walks by. "You'll need a ladder to reach above the windows. There's one propped against the back of the shed."

I look over at her. She's still wearing that old black sweater over a faded blue dress that covers her legs almost to her ankles. But what's really odd is the pair of white Nike sneakers that poke out from the folds of the hem. With her silver hair trying to escape the red bandana and the worn clothes, she's the epitome of bag-lady fashion except for the expensive footwear.

"What's with the shoes?" I smile to let her know it's not a criticism.

"Arthritis. They're lighter than the clunky orthos. Besides which they were a gift." She pauses and then stares at me for a few moments without speaking. "You seem a little clearer after your bath. That and the physical labor makes you stronger, more able to resist this evil within you. You'll need every edge you can get, believe me."

"This thing wants to procreate, Margrit. That's why it attached to your cousin Sasha. And now it's targeting me for the same reason." I watch her nod and square her shoulders pulling back.

The next thought is thoroughly depressing. "If I can't get rid of this thing I can never have a girlfriend, never marry, never have any chance of a normal life. I won't be used by this demon to help spawn some monster."

"You're young, Adam. It may take a while to thoroughly exorcise it from you, but don't be so fatalistic." She steps closer and a smile flickers in her eyes. "I'm glad to see you've figured this out on your own. What it wanted with my cousin was abhorrent, and unnatural. We can't let this demon prevail in its plan. We must stop it at all costs." Her face sets in hard lines to emphasize her words.

"And if we can't?" But I already know the answer to that one. I will share the same fate as Margrit's cousin Sasha—I'd die before I'd let this hell spawn procreate using me.

"Sasha was banished by my people. But you are not alone. At first I wanted to run as far away from you as these old feet would take me. But I had a dream the first night you were here. My grandmother and Sasha begged me to help you. If one of us has to die to banish this being... well, I've lived a long life."

"No, Margrit..."

She turns, calling over her shoulder as she walks toward the back stoop. "Paint my house, Adam. Get physically stronger.

Be sure to keep your focus on the task I've given you."

For the first half hour I lose myself in the job, applying even strokes of paint along the graying clapboard with a calm purpose, concentrating on filling the aged grains which suck it up like a sponge. The mechanical repetition is hypnotic.

But then my mind gets bored and starts to wander with random thoughts. My arm muscles, already challenged by splitting the wood that morning fill with a heavy ache. A picture of The Slip, the bar I liked in Watertown, flits through my head and my taste buds tingle, thirsting for an icy beer. I can even hear the chink of the glass under the draft spigot as Sam fills it. The smell of alcohol, perfume, and the old leather chairs tickles my nose. And I can see in the mirror over the bar, a few women coming in for a drink after work or after taking in a movie.

My hand slows, slathering the brush with the white paint and sliding the excess against the side of the can. What I wouldn't give for a cold beer at The Slip. When my other hand raises to swipe a bead of sweat from my brow, my head jerks up.

No.

This is exactly what I'm *not* supposed to be doing—daydreaming about my past life. That life is over, and my job now is to shape up to fight this demon.

Again, I apply the paint, biting the inside of my lip to keep me present in the moment. People have died because of this fiend, and it's up to me to stop it before things get any worse—if that's even possible. Poor Cynthia, Doug, and Lisa.

And Chauncy. Does Mike still have him? I hope so. He's good company for the old guy, and Mike doesn't seem like he's got too many friends.

Shit. Keeping my mind still and concentrating on this job is harder than I would have thought. It's probably the dull monotony of this task, and the paint glistening in the sun isn't helping. Maybe I need a break.

I balance the brush on the edge of the can and then stretch, lurching my way to the back of the house. Unlike this morning after splitting her wood, the old lady hasn't bothered to put out a glass of water or snack. My mouth is dry as dust and my lips are parched.

"Margrit?" I call to the back door. When there's no answer I walk closer about to step up onto the stoop when that invisible barrier thing she put there stops me cold. And there's no sound of any movement inside the house. She's probably dozed off. That's what old people have a tendency to do, right?

I wander over to the driveway, rubbing the knots from my upper arm with my hand. Her car glints in the waning rays of the sun and I absently round it to the driver's side, checking out the worn upholstery and dashboard. The old jalopy was probably made more than twenty years ago from the style of it. I try the door and when I find it unlocked, I get inside. There's almost two-hundred-thousand miles in this old...

The key is in the ignition. The dangling plastic happy face sways under it on a chain. Margrit's either really trusting or just plain stupid. There's not many people out this way, but still, you never know, right?

My fingers close over the key and before I know it the motor fires to life. A quick glance at the front door shows that it's still closed. I'd half expected her to come flying out, giving me shit for being in her car and not painting. But there's no sign of life around the house. She might be asleep for another hour or so.

Should I?

The next thing I know I'm backing out of the driveway, already tasting the icy bite of that first sip of beer, the foam coating my upper lip. Just one won't hurt. I never did get a chance to see the small town, and for sure I'd like to see some of it.

Besides, she won't even know I'm gone. I'll be back before the old lady wakes up. I've earned a break from all the hard work I've done around her old house. If she'd left a cold drink for me I probably wouldn't be doing this. And it's not like I can get in her house to use the tap. Just one cold glass of draft beer will do the trick.

Maybe I can find an internet café and check up on Amy, see if she's posted anything on Facebook. Surely Margrit wouldn't be mad if I check up on my sister.

In twenty minutes I'm cruising down the main drag, looking for a hole in the wall bar where I'm not likely to get carded. A flashing Budweiser sign outside a place on a side street catches my eye. I turn down the narrow lane and park the car between two half-ton trucks. I've only got six dollars in my jeans, which is just as well as I can't stay long anyway.

I head over to the wooden door under a striped awning and go inside. The first thing that catches my attention besides the smell of beer is the oversized screen above the bar lighting the dim room with the eerie glow of astro turf and a pitcher winding up to throw a ball. When my eyes get accustomed to the light I wander over, hardly giving a glance to the two women hunched in a booth laughing or the three people shooting pool at the back of the room. I just want a beer, so baaad.

When the bartender, a blowsy woman in a too-small, white T-Shirt, her blond hair high and tousled wanders over, I ask, "What's on tap?"

She shifts a wad of gum to her cheek and smiles. "Bud, Busch, and Coors." Her eyes meet mine and for a moment I freeze. Asking for ID hovers in her mind but then disappears in a flash.

Acting as casual as you please, I slide onto the stool and glance up at the monitor above her. "I'll have the Coors, please."

She saunters off and glances over as she holds the glass under the tap. "Hot day out there, huh? You're new in town."

"Yeah. Just finishing a painting job, needed a cold drink." I try to avoid eye contact as much as possible, yet I know she's still glancing over, trying to engage me in conversation. The woman is in her forties, bored, and she's got a kind of dreamy look in her eye, glancing at me. Oh my God. Not another Lisa. What is *with* these women? If she were maybe ten years younger, I might consider it but...

She's barely set the drink down in front of me, lingering while I fish out a couple bills to pay for it, when the other two women leave their booth to sit next to me. I plunk the bills down, but the bartender makes no move to take it.

The woman on my left sidles closer, so close that the faint odor of cigarettes wafts from her skin. She's got dark hair and sky-blue eyes outlined in liner so thick it's clumped and flaking off in chunks. "What's yer name? Can I buy you a beer?"

I stare into my beer and mumble, "Adam."

This is totally crazy! I can feel all three of them shifting closer to me. I'm sensing the lust in their gazes as if I'm some kind of Tom Cruise, which I'm absolutely not.

The one on the right actually places her hand on my thigh, stroking higher with each second that passes. "If you're Adam, then I'm *Eve,* if you get my meaning."

The bartender bends, placing her elbows on the bar in front of me, displaying a generous view of cleavage. "I'm off at nine if you're interested in getting together."

I look up at her. "Sorry. I've just got time for one beer."

The cigarette mama leans closer still. "Where are you off to? I can keep you company." Her fingers brush along the back of my hand and linger.

This isn't right. These women normally would look past me, yet here they are practically throwing themselves at me. I gulp half of my beer and set it down. "Thanks, but no."

The one on my right gets so close my chest tightens, feeling suddenly claustrophobic.

My voice is a growl, "Look, I'm not interested. Can you give me some space here?"

But this has the opposite effect on them. They're practically fawning over me, touching me, their perfume and breath wafting off in waves.

"Hey! Leave me alone! I'm gay, studying for the priesthood, celibate, whatever! How 'bout we leave it at gay-celibate—anything! Just let me alone, okay?" I spin around and storm out of the bar.

Shit! It's happening again. There's no doubt what made

them so attracted to me. It's that demon that's controlling them, just like in the bar with Cynthia. Look how well *that* turned out.

Why the hell did I come into town? I should have known better. But the thing is, after leaving the back of Margrit's house, things are kind of fuzzy. But that scene in the bar acted like smelling salts, jolting me back to reality.

The light outside makes me squint and for a moment I'm disoriented. Where the hell did I park the car?

A high-pitched wail, and the sounds of boys yelling catch my attention. It's coming from down the street. Some kid is getting his ass kicked by bullies. I race toward the wails and laughter and see four boys aged thirteen or so in a circle pushing a smaller kid. The kid's crying, trying to keep his glasses on as they jostle, thrusting him from one side to the other.

"Hey! Let him go!" I bolt to the first guy—the biggest—and spin him around to face me.

"Fuck off! This ain't your business!" His eyes are slits as he yanks out of my grasp, joining his friends.

That's it! I can barely see when the blinding rage hits me. I grab him by the back of his collar with one hand, spinning him around to land a solid blow in his gut. He folds over and my knee reacts with a solid thrust upward into his face. The sound of bones crunching is music to my ears.

One of his friends jumps me from behind while the other two are at each of my sides belting me with blows to my arms and shoulders.

My arm raises to wrap over the neck of the guy on my back. With a sharp bend he goes flying over and to the side taking out the opponent on my right. They've hardly landed when I strike the other one down, pummeling him with my fists. He's on the ground and I'm on him, beating him till his face is bloody. Blinding rage courses through me.

Another kid comes down the alley. "Stop it! What's going on?" From the shock in his voice I know he's not part of this gang of jerks.

But I can't stop. With every punch to this kid's face, Eric and the guys who bullied me at school feel it. Every humiliation, every taunt and blow they dished out to me is rained down on this punk under me.

The other three run away, but the kid who just entered the alley keeps coming. He throws his body at me, knocking me off the punk. The young thug I was beating takes this opportunity to scrabble to his feet and lurch away, out of my clutches.

I turn on the new kid and before I even know it, I'm lifting him up, holding his leg and torso higher and higher. He flies through the air and into a dumpster hulking at the wall of a building. His yelp of pain breaks through the rage that gripped me in its spell.

The innocent kid, the one who was being picked on, grabs the skateboard the thugs had tried to take from him and darts the other way out of the alley. The look of fear in his eyes stops me cold.

When the last guy peers over the rim of the dumpster I see his aura. Oh my God. This is a good guy who I could have seriously hurt, tossing him into the garbage like a piece of trash. And not just that, but he's gifted like I am—not as strong as me but still it's there. From the look of horror in his eyes when he edges away, stumbling in the refuse bags, I know he sees it, the demon, the darkness that envelops me.

I race back to the mouth of the alley and across the street to where the car is parked. It's a few moments before my hands can stop shaking enough to put the key into the ignition. Oh my God. That demon used my hate, my resentment of being bullied... I almost killed that kid! The kid was a punk, but he didn't deserve to die because of that. Let alone the other boy I just threw in the trash! What happened to me?

After taking a few deep breaths I calm down enough to start the car and drive out of town. This was a mistake, sneaking into town for a beer with Margrit's car. From the time I took a break from painting right up to now, this demon has pulled the strings. That's enough to scare the bejeezus out of me and... Boy oh boy, the old lady is going to have a fit. I'll be lucky if she doesn't throw me out on my ass.

She warned me, and I wasn't strong enough to resist it.

I sink lower in the seat. I'm not going to make it. She's going to give up on me and I'm doomed. And I can't blame her. I'm radioactive to anyone around me because of this poison inside me.

'You give me too much credit.'

Oh shit. To make matters worse, the voice is back to gloat.

"Why? Why can't you just let me go?" I swab a tear trickling down my cheek away with the back of my hand.

'And miss this fun? You have to admit that pulverizing that punk's nose to a smear was satisfying, Adam. He deserved to die.'

"No! I told you, NO MORE HURTING OR KILLING!" I pound the steering wheel with my palm.

'Settle down. And just so we're clear... that fight was your doing, not mine. I take credit for the women coming on to you in the bar, but that gang? Not me, bucko. All you. And you liked it.'

This is more horrifying than if it had made me do that. I'm not a bully or a street brawler. "You're lying! That's what you are, a stinking liar. I don't believe you."

It couldn't be true. In all the times I was picked on in school I'd never resorted to violence. It was one of the things that my older brother Seth used to berate me over. He'd even tried to teach me how to fight but I wouldn't.

It couldn't have been me almost beating that kid to death. My gut sinks lower still picturing the blood streaming from his nose, his eye swollen and almost shut from the punches I rained down on him.

And another cold fact sinks in. The kid will tell his parents, who in turn will tell the cops, and they'll have a pretty good description of me. Coincidentally, this will be a perfect match with the guy they're looking for in a series of murders in Watertown.

I am done for. They'll find me and arrest me. Maybe I should just keep on driving. Why not add grand theft to my list of charges? Can it get any worse?

But the old lady's house comes into view and I wheel the car into the driveway. She doesn't have much and for sure taking her car would be the final straw. She'd never be able to replace it, and living this far out in the boonies without it would be a death sentence.

She's standing on the front veranda, arms crossed over her chest when I get out of the car. The paint supplies are nowhere to be seen. The silver aura isn't as pure as it was when I first saw her. Now it's threaded with gray and red. She's pissed all right.

"Leave my car keys on the walkway." Her voice is cracked and tired. She turns and goes back into her house, closing the door softly behind her.

Somehow, this is worse than if she'd ranted and screamed at me. I've disappointed her and yet she didn't tell me to go. With heavy feet I walk over to the walkway and set the keys just outside the metaphysical barrier.

The sun casts a dim light from where it has set under the horizon. My body aches, and my fist is swollen and throbbing from the fight. I don't think I've ever felt lower than I do at that very moment. The only thing I managed to do right was walk away from those women in the bar. But it's a small victory in view of the street brawl, almost killing that kid.

I look at the dim light shining from her house. This is a good woman who's trying to help me. Even though she is scared to death to even be *around* me, she has the goodness to give it a try. I don't deserve her kindness.

The walk to the shed to lie down for the night is like plodding through quicksand—every step a struggle. This demon is winning the war. It's insidious and sneaky, using every weakness I have to its advantage.

If I stay here like this, I may end up hurting or even killing the old lady.

Tomorrow I have to leave, for her sake if nothing else.

SEVENTEEN

A clanging racket jolts me from a sound sleep. The light shining in the dusty panes of the lone window in the shed almost blinds me when my eyes open. And that metallic banging sound keeps going, shooting pain through my already aching head. I get up and throw the door open.

The old lady is on the back stoop hitting a cast iron skillet with a metal mallet. Her hand holding the mallet lowers and there's a grim set to her mouth, before she calls out, "Good! You're up."

"I'm sorry Margrit about yesterday, taking your car. I'll clear out of here once I get my bag packed." Sighing, I turn to go back into the shed. I'm not sure where I'll go but I can't stay here.

"*Of course.* That's what you *do,* isn't it, Adam? Whenever you have a setback, you run away. But you can't run from this beast. Flight won't work. You must take a stand and fight or you're doomed. If you walk down that driveway, so help me God, I'll shoot you, myself." She drops the skillet and reaching behind her, she lifts a shotgun, pointing it at me.

Even though I know she means every word, I'm not scared

of her killing me. It might be a blessing to end it all.

With a heavy heart, I cry out, "I can't *stay*, Margrit. I almost killed a boy yesterday! I tried fighting it, tried just concentrating on painting, controlling my thoughts, like you said, but it's *too strong*. It led me to that bar in town, and I'm afraid if I stay here, it'll hurt or even kill you."

"Do you not see that this is what it wants? Once more you're playing into its hand, Adam. That evil thing doesn't want you here with me. Yes, it wants you in this town, but definitely not living with *me*." She sets the gun down and then slowly walks down the two steps, facing me.

"I'm partly to blame for what happened yesterday. I gave you more credit for being strong enough to resist than I should have. This beast is a snake in the grass. But I know now what must be done." She starts walking toward me, clutching the stone amulet hanging around her neck. Closer and closer till she's right in front of me.

I back away until my shoulder thumps on the doorframe of the shed. "No. You keep your distance." Even as I say it, it hits me that these are the exact same words she said to me and for the exact reason—to protect her.

She shakes her head and steps closer, putting her arms around my shoulders. It's the first time we've touched.

A sense of calmness seeps into every cell of my body. I fall into her embrace, the tears flowing while my shoulders rack in gut-wrenching sobs. I haven't cried this much since I was a toddler. In that moment I feel all the pain of the past—the fights with my parents, my envy and love of my older brother and of course the sheer sadness of missing my sister, Amy.

Even my friendship with Hilda and with Mike, surprise me in the intensity of how much I miss them.

And then the tragedies of Cynthia, Lisa, and Doug claim me.

It's many minutes of crying unabashedly in this old woman's arms before she eases back. "There. This is a new day, Adam. Now we fight again, *together*." Her fingers dig into my upper arms, and she gives me a little shake to emphasize her point.

It's only at that moment when my tears are shed that glimmers of the old woman's life start to come through. She *is* a fighter, a survivor. She lost her family when the gypsies were rounded up with the Jews and herded off to concentration camps. Her life was spared only because a kind Italian family hid her and then took her in as one of their family.

Her life, marrying a man and emigrating to the USA, their love as they forged a life here, comes through as well. Their final years together were here in this place. There's more than her love in that garden, his ashes are also there.

She eases back and her hands drop, "We have work to do. But first you must eat. From now on you will drink only water and eat only the food which I have grown here. I will not allow you to come into my home... not yet. While I get your breakfast, I want you to sit on that tree stump."

"What? No more wood for me to split? I'm actually going to take it easy?" I'm teasing her of course. There's more that she has in mind for me.

"You are going to focus all your attention on why you deserve to be free of this possession. Too large a part of you has given up already. That has to change."

Her eyes bore through me, seeing things inside me that I've tried to hide for too long. If I've got psychic power, this woman has it as well but in spades. I have to look away from the intensity of her probing gaze.

A part of me flares hotter in anger that she's able to do this so easily. But is it that my insecurity is laid out like a buffet table, or is it this thing inside me which hates her? Hates her goodness and power? It had the upper hand yesterday but now feels the threat of Margrit. It's still infecting me like a virus, but I sense it squirming in the face of the old lady's goodness.

I follow her across the yard and stop at the old oak tree stump. As I settle onto its rough surface, the screen door behind the old woman slams shut. Closing my eyes I try to focus on why I totally don't deserve to be in this fiend's possession. What did I ever do aside from being gifted with paranormal ability to have this demon glom on to me? Why me and not some psychopath who might even like it?

A feeling of calm energy floods through me, and my mind stops spiraling in the whirlpool of pity. I'm better than this. I've been looking at this situation as a *victim*. A victim relinquishes power to another.

I'll be damned if that's going to happen anymore. There *is* good in me along with power. Amy saw it and loved me. She saw past my parent's' and my brother's disappointment in me.

Amy thinks I'm kind of cool actually. But what is cool? Being a smart-ass, perceptive to a fault, and never listening to anyone's advice? That isn't going to cut it.

This is hard stuff for someone like me. I can read auras, know people's deepest, darkest secrets with just a touch, yet when it comes to knowing my own qualities—are there any? I'm muddled except in acknowledging my psychic power.

Okay. Number one, I'm smart. Even my teachers knew that. I can read a history text book and not only learn about important past events but I actually can slip into that scene. It's not like being in a movie, nothing that detailed, but the mood, the people involved come to life for me. Hence I could ace exams if I bothered to actually finish them.

I guess... I'm kind to people too. Well, I don't go out of my way to do harm, that is. Even with Cynthia: when I knew the demon wanted to take advantage of her I bolted. So that makes me sensitive and kind.

This is working! My mind is clearer, and there's a sense of serenity that makes me feel lighter.

I smile, inhaling deeply, but my throat stings. The acrid smell of the air makes my chest tighten.

What is that? I look over at the house to see smoke pouring out the screen door and the window at the side.

Oh my God! The house is on fire! Margrit's in there!

'She thought she could beat me. Well, looks like that will be her last thought.'

Damn it! Somehow the demon did this!

"Margrit! Mrs. Kovacs? Get out of there!" But I know she's

out cold. There's no sense of her presence, not a fragment of her essence anywhere.

I race to the front of the house, hoping against all odds that somehow she's lifted that barrier and I can get inside to get her out.

EIGHTEEN

My heart pounds as I race from the stump and over to the back step. But as soon as my foot lifts to go up I'm bounced back like I've just hit a wall.

Damn it! That crazy barrier she put there is keeping me out. I've got to get in there somehow.

"Margrit! Mrs. Kovacs! Can you hear me?" The smoke is becoming more dense, and there's a glow of the fire flickering in the glass of the window.

What's worse is that I know she's unconscious. There's no glimmer of her essence in the house. Somehow that demon managed to set her house on fire and I can't get in to help her!

Even though it's a long shot, I race to the front of the house to try getting in the front door. But, again her barrier keeps me away.

The window! Maybe she hasn't put any protection on it. I can get the ladder and break in. I run to the back of the shed. "Please let this work!"

Grabbing the ladder, I sprint back to the house, all the while watching the smoke rolling and banking out through the back door. My hands shake as I prop it against the house, next to the window. Praying that this will work... praying I'm not too late to save her, my feet fly up the rungs.

I'm halfway up, reaching to the open window to see if I can get through, when the sound of a vehicle, tires crunching on the gravel in the driveway catches my attention. A rapid glance shows that it's a truck with some chick driving it. But there's no time to think about that.

The old lady will suffocate soon if I can't get in. My hand darts out to grab the edge of the window but it's like it hit a hard rubber ball, bouncing back before it even touches the glass.

Damn it, Margrit! Another barrier spell. How am I—

"Oh my God! Mrs. Kovacs!" The young woman runs up the driveway, her brown hair streaming behind her. She races up the front steps and disappears into the house without another word.

Now my heart is skipping beats as I cling to the ladder.

It's surreal. That girl. That girl was the one I saw in my dream at the churchyard. She's even wearing the pink sundress. What the hell?

I almost fall from the ladder watching through the window, catching glimpses of her through the smoke-filled room. She's got the old lady's arms draped over her neck as she struggles to lift both of them to their feet. And then the smoke clouds my sight.

At the sound of footsteps and coughing from the front veranda, I jump from the ladder to go help. The teenage girl stumbles across the floor of the veranda, almost falling down the steps but still holding Margrit up. Her eyes are filled with tears as she strains, the lean muscles of her legs smudged with soot.

Margrit keels over at the waist, hand clutches her throat while long hacking coughs bark from her mouth.

Thank God. She's breathing!

I race to the old woman and ease her down onto the step. Before I even can say a word the young woman bolts back into the house.

"Wait! Don't go in there!" I try to go after her but of course the barrier flings me back. "Shit!" I can only stare at the empty opening, hoping she comes out soon. The smoke in there... Oh God.

Margrit hunches over, wheezing and gasping air into her lungs. She grabs my arm, gazing into my eyes with horror. "It happened so quick. The pan of eggs and the bacon just went up in a flash! How?" The way she looks at me needs no words.

We both know that this was no accident. That fire was set by the demon. Somehow it got into her house to kill her and it almost succeeded—would have—if not for the young woman showing up when she did.

Margrit stares at the door and yells, her voice crackling, "Leah! What are you doing? Come out!"

The girl appears in the opening, a smudge of soot and ash on her forehead, her hands blackened, coughing, but managing to get the words out between gulps of air. "It's out. I doused the flames, but I'm afraid your kitchen's a disaster, Mrs. Kovacs."

Her eyes narrow, reflecting the same gray as thunder clouds when she glares at me. "Why didn't you help her?" Her chin in a heart-shaped face raises higher, and her mouth is a straight line when she steps closer to me. "Who *are* you? Did you do this?"

I jerk back seeing her fingers close into fists at her sides. "No! I was trying to *help* her!"

"By watching her through the window? Big help! She was barely breathing when I got to her." She turns, tucking her long hair behind her ears, lowering to hug Margrit. Her features soften, revealing beauty in the concern she shows for the old woman. "Are you okay? We should take you to the hospital."

The old lady pats the girl's thigh. "I'll be okay if I can just sit here for a few moments. Can you get me a drink of water, Leah?"

"Let *him* go for water. I wanna stay with you to make sure you're okay." She throws another foul look my way before turning once more to Margrit, holding the old lady's hand in hers.

She's a total contradiction. One minute a total bitch glaring at me and the next, an angel in her concern for the old lady. I take a seat on Margrit's other side and lean over, scowling at this Leah beeyotch. "I can't! Don't you think I would if I was able? You'll have to go!" I can't believe this is the same young woman in my dream. Maybe it was a nightmare.

"Is there a piano strapped to your back? Is that why you're so useless?" She spits the words, practically fuming as she stomps off into the house.

Trying to ignore bitch-girl, I turn to the old lady. "I'm so sorry, Mrs. Kovacs. I should have left when I said I was going to." I hunker closer to her, examining her face and hands for any burn marks. I'd known something bad would happen to the old lady for helping me. This is all my fault.

"No! If I catch you blaming yourself anymore for this... this *Hell Spawn's* actions, I swear I'm going to give you a swat!"

Leah steps out of the door. "I knew it! I knew he had something to do with this!" She hands the glass of water to Margrit and then as she's stepping over to continue the verbal assault, her sandal catches on a loose board on the veranda. The bitchy scowl drops almost as quickly as she stumbles.

Before I know it, I'm up and grabbing her arm to steady her and prevent a nasty fall down the steps.

The contact with her flesh makes me seriously wish I hadn't touched her. Oh my God. Leah's shrewish mother, her henpecked father, and a picture of her brother flood through my mind in that instant. The worst of it is that the kid I tossed in the dumpster... Oh shit. It's her *brother,* Preston!

"What?" Her eyes flash wide, staring at me with open curiosity. "What's with that look? Do I *know* you?" She yanks her arm away and rubs it like my touch soiled her skin.

"No. It's nothing." I turn away and sit down again beside the old lady, but my mind is working overtime. I was meant to come to the old lady's house—to the old lady who has a protégé—this Leah chick. A protégé with zero paranormal talent but who's trying her best to acquire it. Maybe she thinks if she hangs around Margrit some of the old woman's power will rub off on her?

Not likely.

Margrit finishes the glass of water and hands it to me. "Be patient with her, Adam. She's a good person."

"What are you *saying,* Mrs. Kovacs? I don't need you to defend me to this guy, this useless creep who wouldn't even lift a finger to help you when you were out cold. You could have died." She directs the question at the old lady but her eyes never leave me. "Who is this guy and what's he doing here? Is he a relative or something?" Leah stands with her arms tightly crossed over her chest. The resentment she feels for me comes off in flaming red waves.

"Help me to my feet, Leah." Margrit takes the hand that Leah extends and rises, shooting a sad look at her. "You can't stay here, Leah. I'm grateful you showed up when you did, but it's not safe for you to be here."

Leah's mouth falls open but then she recovers quickly. "It's because of *him,* isn't it? I don't think it's safe for *you* to be alone out here with him. Hell, you might be dead if I hadn't come along."

I can't stay silent, especially now that I've made the series of connections. This is playing out like a well-thought-out blueprint. And the architect hasn't revealed the final draft. I look at her. "Why did you come out here, Leah?"

Her eyes are flinty when she looks at me. "What's it to you? Mrs. Kovacs is my friend. I usually come out on the weekend to see her. Not that it's any of *your* business."

"So, no sudden urge?" This is going to make me sound like an egomaniac but I have to ask, "You aren't *attracted* to me?" I look at her. I mean *really* look into her depths, her aura to see for myself.

"Oh my God!" She throws up her hands, unable to say anything more she's so flabbergasted. But there's no lie in what I see inside her. She really did come out to see Margrit, and the animosity she feels for me isn't masking any attraction whatsoever.

Huh.

Leah shows that she's never at a loss for words for long when she speaks, "Are you that out of touch with reality? You think I'd be attracted to *you*? As if. Wow! You've got some serious issues with your self-image, jerk."

Now it's my turn to get hot under the collar. This neophyte, this dilettante, wannabe psychic has no idea. "Lately women have been falling over themselves to get next to me."

Her lips form a nasty sneer. "Cause you're such a hero, I guess."

This verbal ping-pong match is getting us nowhere. I look at Margrit to see if she has any ideas why this Leah would be immune to the demon's tricks, making her unlike the others who came on to me in a big way.

She shrugs but she's still wary of letting Leah be anywhere close to me until we've exorcised this entity. Again, she turns to Leah. "Go. It isn't forever Leah, but right now you need to leave Adam and me alone."

Leah grasps Margrit's arm, leaning closer. "I don't trust him, Mrs. Kovacs. Let me stay. I'll clean the mess in your kitchen and make you something to eat. I don't feel right leaving you alone with this guy."

Much as I hate to admit it, she has a point. If she hadn't come along, Margrit could be dead.

And for whatever reason, she's immune to the demon's machinations. Aside from Margrit, Leah is the only woman who hasn't thrown herself at me. She's either able to resist, or I'm more repugnant than I care to admit. I kind of hope it's the former not the latter reason.

Still, I have to agree with Margrit. This being is sneaky. The fact that Leah was in my dream is the final penny dropping. "I'm not going to hurt Margrit. She's trying to help me. If you stay you'll wreck everything. Nothing personal Leah, but you need to go."

She turns on me, leading with her chin. I have to admit it, but with her delicate features, it's kind of cute. "How do I know you're not a serial killer, some kind of arsonist? What's your last name? I've got cop friends, and I might just ask them to check you out."

"Marshall. Adam Marshall." It just popped out; my mother's maiden name. There's no way I'd tell her the truth, not with the APB that's probably out on me.

"Got any ID to prove that?"

My God, the girl's a bulldog with a bone! But Margrit settles the matter. "Enough, Leah! I trust Adam and that should convince you. After all we've been through—"

She spun on her heels facing Margrit down. "All *you've* been through? Remember who was the one who actually helped you, Mrs. Kovacs. That was me!" Again she turns the third degree on me, arms crossed actually tapping her toe on the hard-packed walkway. "How long have you been here? When are you leaving? WHY are you here?"

I step into her space, barking my answer, "I've been here a couple days, and it's none of your concern when I choose to leave. The *why* is absolutely none of your business." Although I am getting the strong feeling that it totally concerns her. She is somehow tied into this demon's horrid plan.

Mrs. Kovacs' knees actually creak when she steps between us, hand up like a traffic cop's. "Enough!" But she turns a hard gaze at Leah. "I'm not asking you to leave, Leah. I'm ordering you. GO!"

Leah is silent for a few beats glaring at both of us before she bursts out, "Okay. Okay. I'm leaving. But I'll be back." There is challenge in her narrow eyes when she looks at me. "I don't trust you, buster. If anything more happens to Mrs. Kovacs you'll have *me* to deal with. Got it?"

I nod and watch her storm down the walkway and then get into the car, slamming the door shut. There's no doubt in my mind that she means every word she spoke.

Unlike the demon who promised no one else would be hurt. But that's in its nature, of course—a deceiver and a liar.

Mrs. Kovacs hands the empty glass to me. "Take this in and get me another glass of water, would you? I need to sit in the fresh air for a spell."

"I can't. You have that barrier thing there."

"I cleared the spell while you two were throwing a hissy fit, fighting like a pair of cats. There's carrot bread on the table. Bring it out too, if it's not charred to bits. I'll be out back, thinking. This is going to take a while. I need to sit and ponder."

NINETEEN

Slowly my foot rises to rest on the bottom step and I smile when it stays there. After getting bounced back like a yo-yo so many times I am half expecting it to happen again despite Margrit's assurance. The small entranceway branches off to a sitting room on the right and a large, smoky kitchen on the left. At the end of the hallway is the old lady's bedroom and a bathroom. The place is gloomy and even smaller inside than what it looked like from the yard.

I enter the kitchen and see the blackened pans and the stove covered in black ash. Some of the flash fire charred the cabinet next to the stove and curled the laminate countertop. The pale yellow walls are streaked brown from the smoke damage. Spying the carrot bread, I grab it and a knife. The only thing left is getting water for the old lady. I find the pitcher she had the other day and fill it from the tap.

When I go out, Margrit is perched on top of the tree stump where she told me to sit. She's hunched over, looking ancient and totally worn out. This is taking more out of her than she'd expected. The fact that her spell protecting the house isn't enough to keep the demon out is really shaking her confidence.

Hell, it sends a shiver through my shoulders too.

She looks up as I approach and her voice is sad. "This stump holds the power of the earth. It was an old tree, one hundred feet high when Alf and I moved here. One night it was struck by lightning, sheared in two right down to this stump. We were lucky it never fell on the house. My husband worked for three days cutting it up." She pauses for a few beats reliving those days and continues, "Now, when I'm confused or lonely this spot rejuvenates me."

She looks over at me. "Did you feel its power when you were meditating?"

It's hard to even think about the state of my mind after all that's happened, but I try. After a few seconds pass, a feeling of serenity and power fill my mind. "Yes. I felt it."

She takes the glass I extend to her and smiles. "The feeling is what matters. You might not remember the place or day of your first time riding a bike, but you never forget the feeling. The freedom and joy. And that is what our lives really amount to—a collection of emotions." After she drains half the glass, she continues, "That is part of what this demon envies in us. We *feel* life."

My gut tightens, and I hunker down on the ground next to her. "Which brings us back to the problem at hand—how to repel this demon. It's getting more desperate. Why else would it attack you?"

"Exactly. Slice off some of that carrot bread, will you?" One hand grasps the stone at her neck and she looks pained. "We need to stay together from now on. I see this evil swirling inside you and I sense its frustration with me. But if it's in you, at least it isn't attacking me."

I hand her the slice of bread but her words haven't given me much hope. "But we've got to act fast. What happens when you go to sleep and your guard is down? What's to prevent this thing from finishing you off, Margrit?"

She snorts and almost chokes on the mouthful of bread. "Too bad it was food that caught fire in the kitchen. If it was sage or cedar it would have been a cleansing smudge. When I finish eating, we're going to try that. But this time, I'm smudging *you*."

"That's all it takes? Why didn't you do that yesterday?" I know it can't be that simple, or she would have done it already.

"You need to have your head in the right place, boy. That's why I had you painting, chopping and meditating, earlier. You must be clear in your intentions. To rebuke this evil entity, there must be no hesitation on your part. Your focus must be laser sharp without a trace of doubt or fear." She munches on the bread as casually as if we were discussing how to make soup or weed a garden. She's calm and steady in her mind. Her aura has once more expanded, shimmering in a silvery haze.

"And if I'm not?" But I don't need to hear her answer; I know it deep in my bones. I'm doomed. It would be twice as strong in its power over me.

I look into her ancient, dark eyes, speaking softly, "You can see my aura. You'll be able to judge when I'm ready to do this. But I'm not there yet. That's it, right?"

She nods, and her smile is encouraging. "I'm helping you, Adam. Together we are a formidable pair. Eat and then we smudge you with cedar and sage. That's not the total fix to get rid of this beast, but it's a tool to be used. Think of it as armor. Sage smudging will clear out some of the fear and darkness that is uniquely Adam. We don't need to give that thing, that demon, any tidbits to feed on and grow. We all have some level of doubt and fear. Survival depends on it. But right now, your survival depends on getting rid of what we can."

As I bite into the carrot bread, she sits back and her eyes close. Her lips move softly, but no sound comes out. It comes to me that she's invoking help from her ancestors, saying a chant that she learned from her grandmother. Whatever will help in this fight, is okay by me.

When I finish the bread, her eyes pop open wide and she smiles. "Ready?"

"Yes."

She gets up, and we go into her house. The things she needs are in a small cabinet in the corner. I stand waiting for her to begin the ritual but she laughs.

"Not here, Adam. We're going to the lake. First you bathe. When you're finished I will anoint and smudge your body. We will invoke the power of the four elements—water, earth, fire and air." She holds up a stone fixed to a leather strap. It's black, an exact replica of what she wears. "This will help keep you protected once we do this."

It's a much slower walk to the lake as I help her get through some of the denser underbrush in the forest. Her strength and calm inspire me, and for once my mouth is still. I use this time to try to clear my mind. But the habits of a lifetime don't drop that quickly. It's not long before a picture of my mother sneaks into my head, the disappointment in her tight lips make me sigh with resignation. She always doubted I could stick with anything.

At Margrit's sharp tap on my arm I jerk back. Her jaw works and she clucks her lips, watching me.

Immediately, I straighten, and a sense of calm purpose flows through me. Without another word she turns and continues walking. Just a look from her, and her peace and strength nourish my spirit.

This woman is powerful and pure. She's reached a point in her state of mind that is assured and confident. I can almost feel this darkness that clings in the recesses of my head recoil and become smaller. This demon wants only its own pleasure and gain. It can't face this woman's strength and altruism. I'm witnessing good versus evil and I can't help but feel lighter knowing that kindness is prevailing in this struggle.

'Forgiveness is freedom.'

I look at her recognizing that she has sent that thought into the universe, but it's meant for me. Forgiveness?

Like an air bubble swirling to the surface of a pond a picture of the guys picking on me when I was in school pops into my mind. The fear and shame that I felt so many times by their taunts and jabs makes my stomach tighten, living it as vividly as when I was a child.

I stumble when the recent scene with the bullies yesterday

leapfrogs on to this recollection. My fingers curl in a muscle reflex, remembering the blows I rained down on that punk in the alley.

'Forgiveness is freedom for you, Adam.'

I startle at her voice in my head. She stares at me with a small smile twitching her lips. But this is hard, too damned hard. Tears of anger sting my eyes when I see Eric Holden's sneer daring me to get up and fight back.

His face transforms, and the sneer softens to sadness. It's then that I realize he was projecting the abuse he'd suffered at the hands of his brutish father on to me.

For the first time the ache in the back of my neck melts and my eyes close. Eric and all those jerks who teased me had problems. It didn't make it right to pick on me, but at least I didn't have to go home and get that kind of punishment on a daily basis.

Margrit pauses and her hand rests lightly on my arm. "Let it go. What happened yesterday isn't who you are, Adam. That creature used your weakness, the humiliation and rage you felt as a child to punish the boys in that alley. You aren't that child anymore. You're an adult. Forgive and move on to be free of it. Remove the need for revenge that this cruel beast has used as a weapon."

I feel tension borne of resentment and anger drift from my body. For a few seconds I am weightless, anchored only by Margrit's light touch on my arm. A smile flashes in her eyes before we continue on in silence.

When the lake comes into view, it's almost blinding seeing the sparkles gleaming on the small waves from the sun above. There's an element of the surreal with what we're about to do. How can it be possible in a scene so idyllic, that a darkness, a hateful, I demonic evil can also linger here? The pure light of the day should be enough to banish it. But it's not.

"There's no one here but us, Adam. You can remove your clothes and go to the water. Take as long as you need; I'll be right here." She wanders over to a boulder a few feet away and then sits, watching the lake.

I bite the smart-ass quip back about 'not peeking' and just peel my clothes off. Hell, she's going to be touching me during this ritual so I'd better not get all self-conscious about being naked. Still, I'm glad she's as old as my grandmother, not someone like Leah.

That would get awkward.

Again, the coldness of the water numbs my skin within seconds when I submerse myself. I stay under for as long as I can. "'Peace"' is a mantra that rings with each beat of my heart. When I rise, I feel my body's rhythm quicken while my senses take in everything—the faint odor of the seaweed clinging to rocks, the brightness of the sun and the green shimmer surrounding the trees bordering the shore.

This is life the way it should be—the air so clean, the sun so bright, and the sky an azure blue. There is no place in this world for the dark creature that longs to insert itself into this realm. This is it. I've had it with being this creature's tool. I'm strong and a decent human being, not some victim. I take a deep breath and square my shoulders walking from the cool water over to where Margrit now stands.

I'm ready.

My footsteps are sure when I walk over to her. Her hands rise, showing palms darkened with soil that she smears in a line from my forehead to my chest. She reaches into a bag looped over her neck and again her hands drip with moist earth. Her hand slows as her fingers roll over the marks left by the demon on my stomach and thighs. All the while my heart pounds fast at her healing touch.

"I rebuke you, demon. You took my cousin, but you will not have this boy. Leave him now." Her hands glide over my legs and then she straightens. Again she refreshes the earth on her palms before smearing my arms.

I open my mouth to repeat her words but she shakes her head. "Not yet, Adam. Let me finish." She takes a bundle of grass and twigs from her satchel and sets fire to the end, blowing on the flame until the ends glow a bright orange.

The smell is sweet with the cedar but also acrid, when I

inhale. My eyes close as she continues waving the smudge over every area of my body.

"You are not welcome here, demon. Leave this boy and never come back." Her voice is strong and steady, repeating the words over and over as she continues the ritual.

At the touch of her slipping an amulet over my head, my eyes open. She smiles. "Enough for now. Your aura is clear."

My heart skips a beat at her words. "It's gone?" When she pulls back and nods, I feel like hugging her.

"I think we should repeat this every day for a week. You will be able to tell this demon to leave and there will be no doubt as to your authority. That will be the final step. For now, it's beaten. This battle is won, but remember, we're in a war, Adam." She turns and starts gathering the items to put into her satchel.

It may be a small victory, but it gives me hope that I'll soon be through with this. I hurry getting dressed, totally not caring that my body is caked with mud. It's another level of protection against this beast and I'll take all the help I can get.

My stomach rumbles reminding me I've only eaten a piece of bread with some water. When I join her on the way back from the beach to her house, I turn to her. "How about I make us some lunch after I clean up the mess in your kitchen? It's the least I can do after all your help."

She stops abruptly and her hand jerks up, silencing me. "Adam. It's not safe for you back at my house."

"What? You're throwing me out after all this... just when we make some progress?" But a deeper look into her eyes tells me everything.

Leah has followed through on her threat to go to her cop friend. They're waiting for us at Margrit's house.

TWENTY

What should I do, Margrit? I'm going to be arrested if they catch me. Three people are dead and I'm the link among all of them. The demon butchered them, but there's no way they're going to believe that!"

Oh my God! I'm done for. It's not just getting arrested and going to prison for something I didn't do, it's knowing that I'm still not out of the woods as far as this demon goes.

Yeah. Out of the woods is pretty apt considering I'm standing in a forest about half a mile from her house. But even if I run, what chance do I have of surviving? If the bears or wolves don't eat me first, the cops will send out a search party to comb the area.

"You don't have any choice, Adam. I'm sorry that Leah felt she had to do this. If we'd been honest with her, she might not have. I'm to blame for this. I shouldn't have dismissed her threat." The old lady looks as defeated as I feel right then.

"Damn it! We didn't tell her for her *own* protection! Now look at the mess she's made." If I could get my hands on her... But this isn't getting me anywhere. There's no escape, and I have to face that sad fact.

When the house comes into view, sure enough, a cop car is there along with Leah's truck parked in the driveway.

Margrit places her hand on my arm, making me pause. "I know the policeman. He's a reasonable man but you should let me do most of the talking. I'll say I ran into you in town and hired you to help me get some things done around the house."

It's not that far a stretch from the truth but that part isn't the one I'm worried about. It's the *before* which will land me in a jail cell.

She continues, "As far as what happened in Watertown, you should tell the truth."

"What? Tell them the demon killed those women and my roommate? That's gonna get me admitted to a psych ward, Margrit." She might be wise in the ways of the paranormal, but this is the real world and the truth is not going to cut it.

She shakes her head and continues walking. "His name is Jake, and he's a good man."

"Yeah, but he's not crazy, right? No way is he going to believe a word I say!" I shake my head. "I wouldn't believe this shit if someone tried to tell me about it!"

She stops and takes my arm. "You're mistaken, Adam." Tilting her head toward the cop and Leah The Snitch, she says, "Jake has dealt with strange things, my boy. More than once." She makes a small smile. "If there's one policeman in this world who would give you the benefit of the doubt, it would be him."

I shake my head slowly. "Yeah. Right." For the love of Pete, I don't even think Mike Drogan is a hundred percent convinced I'm innocent anymore. Particularly after I lit out from Watertown after finding Doug's body in our apartment. And he *knows* I am gifted! This cop? Forget it—I am done for.

She gives my arm a jerk, seeing the hopelessness in my eyes. "Adam!" she hisses. "I'm telling you the truth! Jake is not your enemy—he very well may become an ally in all this!"

I scoff. "Not after the smoke Leah's blown in his ear!"

Now Margrit chuckles. "There's a reason she brought him here, Adam. Both of them have had experiences with the unseen world around us."

"Oh yeah?"

"Yes." She looks away for a brief moment. "It was how we all became friends." There was a story there, but before I could ask, she turned to look at me sharply. "Now listen to me. Just stick to the truth rather than tangle yourself up in more lies."

The cop starts walking toward us. His gaze is firmly focused on me even though he extends an arm taking Margrit's satchel and stepping between us. "Margrit. From what Leah said about what happened here I'm surprised to see you out walking through the forest. Are you okay?" He keeps peering at me as he speaks, focusing on the mud smeared over my face and arms.

"Jake, I'm fine. Adam and I walked to the lake. You heard about my kitchen fire, I'm sure." She directs the last comment at Leah who follows close behind the cop.

"Adam Marshall?" The cop jerks his chin up. "You go on ahead where I can keep an eye on you. I'm going to need to see some identification."

Leah's eyes narrow, shooting me a snarky look as she steps closer to Margrit. The pure bitchiness in her face is the final straw.

"Thanks for calling the cops, Leah. What's the matter? Jealous that maybe I'm going to take your place with Margrit? The thing is though, I'm the real deal while you're just a wannabe."

"At least I'm not caked with dirt. What happened? You fall in a mud puddle or something?"

Ignoring her, I put some distance between me and the cop and then turn to him. "My name's Adam Rafferty. I've got identification in my knapsack in the shed. I'll go get it." I start to sprint over but the cop's voice stops me cold.

"Hold on." He hands the satchel to Leah and then his fingers rests on his holster as he strides over. "Keep your hands where I can see, 'em, Adam. And bring the bag out slowly."

I lift my arms higher, turning slightly to face him. There's no doubt he wouldn't hesitate to shoot me if I make a wrong move. But he's also a seasoned veteran from the calm confidence in his movements and voice.

"Sure, Jake. Whatever, just don't shoot me, k?"

"That's Deputy Whittaker to you, kid." He steps closer but keeps an arm's length distance between us.

"Deputy Whittaker, I'm going in real slow, keepin' my hands up. I'm not armed and I don't have any weapons in my bag." My words are calm and steady. This can go bad real fast and I'm the one who'll die.

Margrit rushes over, shaking her finger at him like he's a little boy. "Jake Whittaker! Please. Adam's not a criminal! Do you think I'd allow him on my property if he was dangerous? You understand that I'd *know* if he was!"

Leah joins in the fray, tugging at the old lady's arm. "Mrs. Kovacs! He didn't lift a finger when your kitchen was on fire! He's tricked you somehow!"

Jake has had enough. He barks at the two women. "Enough! Everyone stand back and stay calm. Just get the bag, and we'll get to the bottom of this, shortly." His eyes never strayed from watching me.

"Okay, Deputy." I step into the shed, keeping my hands high where I know he can see them. He's right behind me watching like a hawk.

I lift the duffel bag and hold it out from my body, walking back out the opening. "Do you want me to get my wallet out, or would you rather do it? Any way is fine by me. I'm not hiding anything in there."

"Unzip it and then empty the contents onto the ground."

I do exactly as he asks and my clothes and wallet cascade from the canvas bag, When he sees that there's no weapon, not even a pocketknife, he nods. "Hand me the wallet, Adam."

Tossing the duffel bag aside, I reach for my wallet and hand it to him. He rifles through the layers and pulls out my driver's license and Social Security card. After eyeing me once again and then the picture on my driver's license he's satisfied.

"Adam Rafferty, right?"

When I nod, Leah blurts out "You said your last name is Marshall!"

Jake waves at her to quiet down. "This your real name?" When I nod he continues, "Watertown, huh? What brings you to Saranac Lake?" He still keeps my wallet in his hand, but his other hand has moved away from the gun holster.

I look at Margrit and she nods, encouraging me to be truthful. My gut tightens but I take a deep breath and blurt it out in a rush. "There was trouble in Watertown and I got scared. Even though I had nothing to do with any of it, I took the first bus out of there. I met Mrs. Kovacs and have been helping her around here in exchange for a place to stay and food."

"What kind of trouble, Adam?"

Oh God. This is gonna sink any goodwill that Mrs. Kovacs' vouching for me has induced in him. "Two women were murdered, and the guy I lived with, Doug, was also killed." I'm about to explain but Leah jumps in.

"Murders! Oh my God! Mrs. Kovacs! You let him stay here! Did you know this?" She's staring openmouthed at the old lady.

"Of course I knew! I also knew he didn't have anything to do with it." She shrugs away from Leah and walks over to Jake. "He's innocent. But someone made it look like he did it. He was meant to come here and meet me, Jake. I need to help him."

Jake's hand rises and he shakes his head, blinking hard. "Hold on!" He looks at me, and with a jerk of his head, he signals for me to go to his car. "I'm running your ID through the system. I read about the murders, of course. You should have stayed to talk to the police, kid. Running like you did doesn't put you in the best possible light."

I walk toward the police car and when I'm about ten feet away, Jake orders me to stop. He walks to the car, watching me as he gets in. Margrit and Leah stand close to the house taking this in. There's no doubt in my mind that Jake is going to arrest me.

'You won't be arrested. Don't be so melodramatic. Seriously. This could all have been avoided if you'd just cooperated. It's not like I'm asking you to do something you wouldn't enjoy.'

Shit! It's back! As if things aren't bad enough, this thing, this evil creature that's put me in this predicament takes this opportunity to resurface. So much for the cleansing ritual! I grasp my head in my hands yelling, "Get out! Leave me alone for 'Chrissake!"

The deputy gets out of the car, and this time the gun is out of the holster. "What'd you say? You're in no position to be giving orders, kid. Especially not to me! You're wanted for questioning in Watertown. No warrant for your arrest, but the detectives handling the murders there want to talk to you. Is there anyone you want to call? Your parents? A lawyer?"

Margrit walks over to me, a look of horror in her old eyes. "It's back. I can see it all *through* you, Adam. It tricked us into thinking we had lessened its power." Her fingers clutch the amulet stone tightly and she stays a few feet away from me.

Jake and Leah watch the two of us like we've lost our minds, which in my case isn't that far from the truth except it isn't lost, it's hijacked.

"Mrs. Kovacs? What's going on here?" Jake's voice is soft, but he hasn't stopped pointing the gun at me.

She turns on him. "He's *possessed,* you fool. What he was afraid to tell you is that this demon is the one responsible for the murders. I am trying to help him exorcise it. That's why we were at the lake and he's covered with mud. It was part of the ritual."

Leah steps forward, her eyes almost popping out onto her cheekbones gazing at me. "Holy cow! Is that true? A for-real demon like in the movies?"

But Jake is anything but impressed by Margrit's revelation. After a massive eye roll he shakes his head. "If this were anyone but you Mrs. Kovacs telling me this, I'd... I'd..."

He grits his teeth so hard I can hear them grind. He whips his head from side to side. "Shit! Not again! Why does this stuff keep happening to me? First the ghost in Alex Bay, then here when these crazy kids used the Ouija board!"

Margrit sidles closer to him, putting her hand on his arm. "You can't arrest him, Jake. Deal with this after we get rid of this demon that's attached itself to him. Just a few more days. You can't bring those dead women and his roommate back to life, but you may be able to help this boy."

He shakes his head again and sighs. "I can't do that, Margrit. Leah was right in calling me. If this demon killed those people, what's to stop it from killing you?"

I blurt out the answer. "It already tried. It set the kitchen on fire, entirely on its own. I was nowhere near any of those people when they were murdered. I have an alibi for where I was when the women were killed. But the demon shot that to hell when it killed my roommate. Don't you see? If you take me into custody, Margrit will be no safer. This brute can act remotely. It's been herding me here with the murders to get its heinous plan underway."

Jake sighs, and he looks like his brain is completely frazzled when he speaks, "Oh. And what is that plan?"

Oh boy. This is gonna be more than a little awkward all things considered. I sneak a look at Leah who is staring with her mouth open wide enough to catch flies.

"It wants me to mate with Leah."

TWENTY ONE

"What?" Leah stumbles back, completely astounded. My face is like a furnace. Hell, I don't need a mirror to know that even my neck is flaming red with embarrassment.

"You can't be serious! Of all the ridiculous pickup lines, that one takes the cake!" Her nose wrinkles like I'm a bad smell.

"It's not *my* idea, Leah. You're not exactly my type, you know." Although she totally is, if not for the nasty attitude. Yeah, gorgeous eyes and slightly athletic, long legs which I love in a woman—but that bitchy mouth... not going to happen.

Jake holds his arm higher, shutting off anymore jibes between us. "Mate with Leah? You mean have a baby? This demon thing wants to have a baby? But why Leah?"

"Jake! Why *wouldn't* it want me?" She throws her hand to her mouth and her eyes goggle. "I mean…" Dropping her hand she shakes her head and screams, "Shit! I'm totally losing it here. A demon has singled me out to be the mother of its offspring. Not a human child, mind you. Welcome to *Rosemary's Baby*."

"What? Who's Rosemary?"

She glares at me. "It was a movie, idiot! I've seen every horror flick ever made! It was—"

"Will you two stop? You're giving me a headache with your catfights!" Margrit snarls at Leah and then scowls over at me.

Jake snorts, his gaze flitting between Leah and me, "Maybe they *should* get together. They sound like an old married couple."

"Jake!"

"You're right, Margrit. I'm sorry. It's just that this is all so crazy; it's making me crazy too. Of course, if my boss knew I was having this conversation, even giving any credence to it, I'd be fired so fast, it'd make your head spin." He bursts out laughing. "Just like Linda Blair in *The Exorcist.*"

I'm living a nightmare, and all this guy can do is bray like a donkey? "Hey! How about you guys just forget you ever saw me and leave Margrit and I to deal with this?"

Leah skewers me with a look. "And miss this demon thing?" She draws back and her palm rises. "Doesn't mean I want anything to do with you, Adam; don't get your hopes up. But I want to see this. Besides, I want to make sure Mrs. Kovacs is safe. I still don't entirely trust you."

Jake leans against the car. "I'm with Leah on that one. There's no arrest warrant on you. You're a person of interest the detectives want to talk to, so technically I can't arrest you. Doesn't mean I trust you, though."

"What?"

Jake does another eye roll. "I told you that earlier. They just want you for questioning."

Wow. I was so convinced he'd arrest me that his words haven't even registered. I can't believe my luck. There's no warrant for my arrest! Maybe Mike had something to do with that.

"You ain't home free yet, kid. But if Margrit thinks she can help you, I'll give her a couple days. But I'm going to be around to make sure nothing bad happens to her."

Margrit pats his arm and thanks him with a small smile. She

then turns to Leah. "Jake is staying, but you aren't. It isn't safe for you here. Maybe now you'll believe me."

Leah shakes her head. "No way. I'm staying if he's gonna be here."

TWENTY TWO

While Jake's on his cell phone talking to his office, Leah comes over closer to me staring at me like I'm some kind of fascinating freak. "So aside from killing innocent people and setting fires, what else does this demon do?"

I tug my shirt higher to show her the scratches that still show on my stomach. "It marked me. It's also made me kind of a chick magnet."

She can't stop the guffaw that bursts forth, "Yeah, right! How come it isn't working on me, then? Which brings me to—why me?"

"There's no accounting for taste, I guess." It's out before I can filter it.

Margrit clucks her tongue at us. "This isn't helping, you two sniping at each other. I would think it's obvious why it chose you, Leah. The beast is trying to mock Christianity. The virgin birth and all that."

I can't help but look at Leah a little more closely. She's a virgin? She's probably seventeen or eighteen and still a virgin. Huh. Not many girls her age can make that claim. Especially with her looks. But the personality. Yeah. It figures. I mentally slap myself in the head. I'm nineteen and I'm one too—who the hell am I to slag her for being one?

For a moment she looks rattled, turning to Margrit. "But it can't actually do that, can it? Make me pregnant like Mary in the Bible?"

I answer before Margrit has a chance. "No. Why do you think it needs me, Leah? It's been leading me here to meet you. But unless this thing totally takes control of me, you don't have anything to worry about." But even as I say these words, a flash of her naked appears in my mind and I have to turn away. Is that the demon putting that there? Shit. I know it is.

Margrit must have sensed the change in me as well because she pulls Leah in next to her. "I'm not asking you to leave, Leah. I'm ordering you."

Leah pulls away and then marches over to where I am, "So, your abilities... are they as strong as Margrit's? Is that why this demon chose you?" She shifts her weight and her arms cross her chest.

"Yes. Margrit's power is more refined, much purer than mine. I usually have to touch things to be able to see them. She doesn't have to." Part of me wants to shut her down so she'll get the hell away from me but another darker part sees her vulnerability. She's obsessed with anything paranormal. She could be used so easily.

"So, what did you sense about me when you touched me earlier?"

There's no hostility from her, yet this is a test nonetheless. I take a breath, purposely avoiding looking at her, "I know your Mom hates the fact you spend so much time out here. She thinks that Margrit practices dark magic like some kind of witch. Your father just tries to stay under the radar when your mom is on the warpath. You have a brother, Preston. He's actually a good kid."

I can't help myself from sneaking a glance. Yeah, her eyes are open wider staring at me. She's convinced now and suitably impressed.

"What else?" She moves closer, and I can smell her perfume, a clean floral scent.

"Nothing. And don't try to touch me to keep playing this game. Because it's not a game, Leah." I move farther away from her.

But she follows like a lost puppy. "Were you always like this? Or did you suddenly find that you could sense things?"

This is more about her than me. She wants to know if she can acquire my abilities. "I was born like this. I got the gift from my grandmother. That's how it works—it's inherited. That's why this bastard chose me. It wants my power in its offspring."

"So have you ever used this power for good? Maybe finding lost children or helping police solve crimes? That could be cool." Her eyes sparkle and she brushes her fingers through her hair.

Oh God. She's probably not even aware that she's flirting with me. I take a good look at her. Is she becoming like the women in the bar, feeling a weird attraction to me? I don't see anything dark in her aura besides the warm earthy tone that usually emanates from her.

"You shouldn't hang around me, you know. You were asked to leave." I step away from her and look over at Margrit, but surprisingly it's Jake who backs me up.

"Leah. Go home. I've got this covered. There's no place for you here. Call me tomorrow, and I'll let you know how things are going."

Leah turns on Margrit. "Fine! I'm leaving! This is the thanks I get for saving you, Mrs. Kovacs? You're trying to help a guy who almost has you killed?" She's ready to explode storming down the driveway to her truck. She opens the door and gives us an angry look.

I glance over to Margrit. The look on her face shows me that she also sees the hurt of being kicked out emanating from Leah. The girl is well and truly pissed off, but her anger is coming from being hurt more than anything else.

Even so, Leah fires up her truck; gravel and pieces of earth fly in the air from her spinning tires as she roars down the driveway to the road.

I breathe a long sigh watching her disappear around the bend. Now that she's gone, Margrit and I need to get back to exorcising this thing. Whatever she did before didn't work, but there must be other ways.

'You're pathetic, Adam. Leah was perfect and you pushed her away. Small wonder you're *still a virgin.'*

It's the final straw for me! But I manage to keep my voice inside my head: *"The only one who's pathetic is you! You kill innocent people and you don't even care! I was supposed to just go along with your twisted plan like some mindless drone, but you made a serious mistake choosing me."*

I turn away from Margrit and Jake when its hissed whisper invades my head again, '*Your parents were right about you, Adam. You're a loser. You could have been part of something great and you are too stupid to realize that.'*

"I retorted: *At least my parents didn't use me like you want to. Even my brother never used me! I'm nothing less than a piece of fly shit to you. You're a monster, and I absolutely rebuke you! GO from me, back to hell where you belong!*" A blinding pain pierces my temple, and my hands fly up to cover my head.

"Keep resisting, Adam!" Margrit comes closer, placing her palm on my forehead.

I feel the added power and strength flow into me. But the demon isn't done yet.

A throb of psychic power bursts from me and Margrit falls back. Its voice returns in my head, snarling at me. '*I'm going. The only thing stopping me from murdering you and this hag is revenge. What I'm going to do will cause both of you years of suffering!'*

And then it's gone.

Gone.

The strangest sensation floods through me. I swear the only thing anchoring me to the ground is Margrit's hand. Jake joins me in helping the old lady get up from the ground.

Her eyes well with tears looking at me. "You're free! There's nothing dark hovering in your aura now, Adam. You finally found your focus and power to banish that evil within you."

Jake peers at me narrowly, examining me, but I know he's not seeing anything different. "What? It's over?"

Margrit answers him but she beams a smile at me. "Yes. Adam is clear now. He finally had enough and his anger focused him. He cast it out."

But the last threat the demon made, sounds in my head. I turn to Jake. "Can I use your phone, Jake? I need to call my sister and a friend of mine. They may be in trouble."

He fishes his phone from his shirt pocket and hands it to me. "Should I alert the police in Watertown about your sister?"

My fingers fly dialing Amy's cell number. "Not yet. She's in Buffalo with my parents. But I have friends in Watertown." When Amy answers on the fourth ring, I almost collapse on the ground with relief.

"Hello?"

"It's Adam, Amy. Are you at home?"

"Yeah. I just walked in the door. I've been trying to get a hold—"

"Amy! Are Mom and Dad there? Seth? You guys need to stay together. It's important!" My heart is pounding as I picture Doug's butchered body, knowing that my sister may now be in this demon's crosshairs.

"Mom and Seth are here. Why? What's going on?"

Jake grabs my arm. "Give me the address and I'll have a car go there to check on them."

"Lock the door and stay together. I've made an enemy, and you guys may be a target to get back at me. This is really dangerous, Amy."

"But what about *you*? Are you in danger?" Her voice is shaking and hesitant, barely holding back the tears. I know I've gotten through to her and they'll take precautions.

"No. I don't think so. Just stay safe, Amy. I love you."

I end the call and turn to Jake. "It's 42 Palmyra Drive, Buffalo."

When he dashes off to his car to call that in, I dial Mike's number. All the while, Margrit remains still, silently watching me.

Mike answers right away. Thank God.

"Mike. It's Adam Rafferty. I'm in Saranac—"

The volume of his voice almost busts my eardrum. "I know where the hell you are! I was going to drive there tomorrow to find you and bring you back here."

"Wait! I need you to do something for me, Mike! I need you to drive to Buffalo and check on my family. This demon thing has left me, but it might hurt them to get back at me. There's a cop car going over to the house, but they don't know about this demon, Mike. You know what it's capable of."

"Give me the address."

"42 Palmyra Drive."

And then he's gone. Just like that.

Margrit steps closer and pulls me into her, the two of us standing quietly hugging. We've saved me from this possession, but have we unleashed bloody horror on my family?

TWENTY THREE

Jake comes back from making the call on his radio. He's shaking his head.

"What's wrong?" I ask.

"Well… I got my boss on board. He contacted Buffalo PD and they're going to look out for your family." He snorted. "I told them that you're a witness to multiple homicides in Watertown and you just got word that the perp is going after your family there." He looked over at Margrit with a funny expression. "It's kind of weird."

Margrit blinked innocently at him, but stayed silent.

"What's so weird, Jake?" I ask.

He turned back to me. "My boss didn't say a word about paperwork on this matter. Usually when we do interdepartmental stuff like this there's a ton of paperwork." He slid his gaze back to Margrit. "He just hopped right to it without a peep."

"That's good to hear, Jake," she said softly. "He must have heard the urgency in your voice."

"I think he had some help in making up his mind, Margrit."

She got a faraway look in her eyes. "Maybe just a nudge,

Jake. No more than that. I'm an old woman."

He snorted again and shook his head. "This is sooo weird. Y'know, arresting drunk drivers and rousting underage drinkers is more my speed, nowadays."

"Oh, Jake!" she waves a hand at him. "Small-town policeman, is that it?" I watch the two of them bantering like two old friends. "You used to be in the FBI! So don't give me any guff about how overwhelmed you are by this!"

My eyes goggle. "You're in the FBI too?"

Jake turns to look at me. "Nope. I quit about a year ago to do this." He plucks at his uniform and badge.

"Isn't that a step down?"

He smiles and looks over at Margrit. "Nope. Not at all. When you meet my wife you'll understand."

Margrit nods. "Jake is doing what he's meant to do, Adam."

He lets out a snort. "Yeah! Lawman ghost fighter!" He shakes his head. "Wait'll Claire and the kids get back from their trip. They won't believe this."

Margrit steps up to him. "Now Jake—you know they'll believe every word." She's smiling as she says it.

I am watching the two of them. They are like old friends—comrades in arms or something like that. There is a history between these two. Margrit holds her arms out from her sides. "Sometimes we have to do difficult things, Jake. Things we' rather not, but which we know are for the greater good, right?"

He waves at her dismissively. "Yeah, yeah…" He cocks an eyebrow at her. "Is this thing with my boss going to come back and bite me in the ass?"

She drops her arms and steps up to him, putting a hand on his chest. "Dear one… if we don't resolve this challenge..." She gestures to me. "Your boss will be the least of our problems."

He rolls his eyes at her and turns back to me. "Buffalo PD will probably assign an unmarked car to watch your family just for a day or two. 'Fraid that's the best I can pull off."

Even so, relief flows over me. I have a feeling all this will be resolved in the next day or so. "Thanks, Jake," I said. "My friend, Mike, in Watertown is going there as well. He's an ex-cop. He's a private investigator now. I had just started working for him when all this shit started going down."

"Oh yeah?" Jake actually smiled watching me. It was the first time he'd done it.

Encouraged, I continued, "The funny thing is, it was the first job I've ever done that I actually enjoyed." It was true. A lot of that had to do with Mike, himself. Even though he was rough around the edges, he was a lot like Amy in how he treated me. He saw my faults, but he also saw the good in me.

"Mike believed me about this demon. He'll watch over my family till I get home." Till I get home. My words kind of surprise me but they come from my heart. I have to do this. It's time to make amends with my parents and brother. Despite everything that has happened between us, I still love them.

"You know you have to talk to the Watertown police. I've got to alert them that you're here."Jake casts a glance over at Margrit and sighs. "I have to, Margrit. It's my job."

She nods slowly. "I know. But I want Adam to stay here for a couple of days. There's a few things I need to teach him about protecting himself from the likes of that entity. This all could have been avoided if he had known more." She turns to me and her eyes are sad. "Your grandmother should have taught you more when she was alive. It's up to me now."

"But my family, Margrit? I've got to get back to them." Even though Mike will be there, I have to see them for myself to be sure they're okay.

"Like Jake said. They'll be protected by the police for a day or two. Plus your friend will be there. This is important Adam. *You're* important in all this." She puts her hand on my shoulder and gives it a squeeze, emphasizing her words.

Jake nods. "She's probably right. I don't know how she does all this, but I believe her."

But what comes through to me from Margrit holds a trace of worry. Worry, that this demon will come back to me. It's devious, which I know all too well.

"Okay. I'll spend the night, and we'll talk about this tomorrow." I turn to Jake. "Do you mind if I borrow your cell phone? I'd like to check up on my family again. I promise to return it when I get into town to catch a bus back."

"Sure. But you can probably catch a ride with the detectives from Watertown. I'm betting they'll show up tomorrow." He starts walking away, calling over his shoulder. "I guess I don't need to tell you to stay put until they arrive."

And he gets in his car and leaves.

Margrit starts to lead the way over to the old stump but I stop her. "I have to call my family, Margrit."

"Yes. Then, we'll begin our lesson. It'll help in your learning if you're not distracted with worry for them."

Amy answers on the first ring, barely getting a hello out before my father's voice blares through, "Adam! What's all this about? You've scared your sister half to death with this talk of enemies. What have you done now?"

My back straightens, and I'm barely able to stop the smart-ass remark, taking a long breath. "I haven't done anything! But I've made an enemy. He's killed people, Dad! Have the police been there yet?"

"Yeah. There's a cop car across the street right now. Who is this guy? The cops couldn't give me any information, aside from the fact there was some kind of tip another cop got." There is silence for a beat or two before he speaks, "Are you okay?"

I can hear my mom in the background asking to speak to me, but Dad continues, "Did this creep hurt *you,* Adam? Are you okay?"

Shit, the fear in his voice goes right to my heart. My breath hitches. "Just a scratch, Pop. But I'm fine, really."

"You sure? You being straight with me?" It had been a long, long time since I ever heard his voice be so… *fatherly.*

"Yeah Dad, I can handle it."

There was a pause again, then he let out a sigh. "You've taken some lumps in life, Adam-ski." That was his pet name for me from when I was little, and it shot straight to my chest. "You're a pretty tough kid when you gotta be." Another pause. "I believe you."

"Really?"

"Yeah. For real. But you need to come home, son. Whatever trouble you've gotten yourself mixed up in, we got your back, okay? All of us."

"I'm fine, Dad. I'll be home in a day or so. There's something I have to do here first." I end the call, fighting tears that sting the backs of my eyes. It's practically the only time I've ever heard my father be anywhere near supportive, let alone understanding. Even Mom sounded worried in the background.

I desperately want to go home, but after all that's happened, I owe Margrit. We need to see this thing through, one way or another. I know in my bones that this demon isn't finished with me, and so does Margrit.

Margrit gestures for me to come over and take a seat next to her on the tree stump. "Come here now. There are things you need to know. You are long overdue in your education."

Walking over to where she is, my fingers flex and straighten, flex and straighten. A big part of me desperately wants to take the next bus to Buffalo to be with my sister. But even Jake said I need to stay put, so here I am.

She turns and looks at me silently for a few beats and then her voice is steady. "You need to believe in yourself, Adam."

"I do. Well... as much as any—"

"No. You don't. At least not to the degree you need to, to survive. Sure, you were angry and the strength and focus of your anger repelled the demon from you. But, I'm talking about a permanent state—a way of *being* in the world."

Again, Margrit is talking in riddles about concepts while I'm concerned with reality, with what that demon might be doing to my sister and family. But I give her some latitude. "How am I supposed to do this? So it becomes my nature?"

She shrugs. "Simple. Have faith."

Okay. Enough. I can't stop the eye roll. "You talk about permanence and faith. How am I supposed to have faith when things can change in a New York minute? This demon shows up, and there are three dead bodies in Watertown. Here one minute gone the next."

"It starts with your family. Who you *are*, Adam."

This time I actually snort. "My family? My father who is actually ashamed of me, or my brother who has always shown scorn? Maybe it's my mother, who, truth be told, feels like I'm her burden to bear, a disappointment."

Margrit's mouth drops and she shakes her head. "You're so full of shit and you don't even know it."

Hearing her swear is surprising, but when she starts laughing, every one of my senses goes into shock. She's braying; her laugh modulating between an ear-piercing squeal and deep thrum of a bass drum. That's not bad enough, but there are tears rolling down her wrinkled cheeks.

Finally, she gets control again but still chuckles as she speaks, "Adam, you can be so foolish. You look but you do not see."

"What's that supposed to mean? Honestly, Margrit—"

"You need the kind of faith that put a man on the moon. The kind that builds towering cities. You need the kind of faith that can change the course of rivers. Faith like a diamond—indestructible."

I can't resist being smart-assed. I look around from side to side. "Oh. Got any lying around you don't need?"

She taps my chest. "You already have it, silly boy!"

I shift away from her, deliberating whether to just leave. "You are totally losing me, Margrit. I don't have anything close to that kind of faith, dammit!"

"Really?" She looks at me from the corner of her eyes with a sly smile. "Are you sure about that?"

"Yes!" I leap to my feet. "Not everyone has that kind of faith, you know! I can't just conjure something like that up out of nothing!"

"You already have it," she repeats.

"I wish I did," I say. I flop back down beside her. "But I don't."

She puts her hand on my arm, stopping me, and her voice is soft. "Adam? Does Amy love you?"

"YES!" The tone of my voice is hard and sure.

Hard as a diamond. My shoulders fall as the penny drops.

I understand.

Whether it's the power of the mystical stump on this ley line or just being near Margrit, a sense of peace settles. I feel myself grow stronger, finally getting what she's been saying.

She continues, "Love. Love is more powerful than fear. Love is more powerful than hate. Love is more powerful than evil."

Just when I start to get it, she's off on another tangent. I sigh, looking at her. "How can you say that?"

She clicks her tongue scolding me and then takes a breath. "Evil, hate and fear are all one dimension." She pauses, acknowledging my blank look and then continues, "You hate the demon, and only the demon. You fear many things, but only one at a time. The most true and raw facet of evil is self-absorption, a single dimension. But love... Love isn't a single, straight line. Love is a sphere which radiates outward in all directions like the sun."

"I'm sorry. But you're losing me on all this talk of spheres, dimensions and the sun while we sit here on a stump."

She pats my knee, "Amy is the nexus of the love sphere. You are in that sphere, but it radiates outward, including your mother, father, brother—all of Amy's friends. It's a sphere. There's depth. Which brings me to that demon."

Now I perk up. This is what I need to know. Finally.

"This is the final lesson for you to understand. That demon creature is a being of fear, hatred and evil. It can threaten you and make you fear, but it wouldn't dare to do battle with Amy. In the light of Amy's pure sphere of love, it would be forced to see how insignificant it really is. It recoils at that kind of truth."

"So you don't think Amy is in danger?"

She shakes her head. "Remember this. When we fear evil and respond with hatred, we give evil power. We can't do that."

Something isn't right and I hit upon it in a flash. "But when we first met, you saw the demon and you were frightened.

Now you're telling *me* to overcome fear."

She grins, pointing her finger at me. "Bongo."

Bongo? Then I get it. "You mean Bingo."

Shrugging. "See? I don't know everything. I'm learning too. When you stop learning, you might as well be dead."

"You were still afraid, Margrit."

She nods. "Yes. And I ran away."

"So? Where does that love stuff protect you?"

"I ran here," she tells me. "In fact, when I came home, I came right to this spot." Margrit pats the tree trunk. "I saw the aura surrounding you, Adam." She closes her eyes and shivers. "I had seen that aura before, when I was a child." Her eyes fly open and she looks at me. "During the war—many of the Nazi commanders had that sort of aura." She sighs. "And like the child I once was, I was terribly afraid and I ran. To here—a place of safety."

I watch her, waiting for her to continue. Layer by layer, she is revealing truths to me.

"Here, in safety, I was able to understand what I was facing. I wasn't sure if you would find me, but I was confident you'd try. So I had to prepare."

I gestured at her home. "The shield you put up."

She nodded. "I wanted to help you, but I had to ensure my own safety first; like a lifeguard swimming out to a drowning man, I needed to make sure I didn't go down with you." She nods to herself. "This entity is powerful, Adam. While I sat here, I recalled all the times I was loved and loved in return." She points to the house. "When I went inside to await your arrival, I went throughout my home, recalling all the love and joy that had been created within. I looked at old photos, handled mementos of our life together…" Her voice fades for a moment. "Shed some tears of longing for my husband…" Her voice brightens. "And was filled with joy and love of my life as it is." She looks at me. "So when you arrived, I was prepared." She pats my hand again. "I was able to help you because of love, Adam—not fear."

I nod. "Love conquers all, huh?"

"Bongo." She smiles and rises slowly. "Enough. Now let's go inside and have some dinner. That is, if the stove still works. And then we rest. Get your things from the shed. You're sleeping on the sofa after you take a shower."

Hmm. Hot water. It's been a while.

I wander over to the shed and grab the duffel bag. My head is still spinning with all that she told me. I cling to the hope that she's right about Amy and even my family. All of this will settle with a good night's sleep.

Little do I know that it isn't meant to be.

TWENTY FOUR

When we come inside, I spend an hour scrubbing Margrit's kitchen down, getting the smoke stains and smell out of her cabinets and walls. Surprisingly, a couple heating elements on the stove still work. After that, I head up to my first shower in what feels like forever. I don't realize how much I miss a hot shower until I step into it. I take my time slathering soap on my body, washing the mud caked on my arms and legs.

At the tap on the bathroom door, I pull the shower curtain back, and my head still layered in shampoo pops out. "Margrit?"

"Adam. Leah's brother Preston is here. You need to finish in there and come out here to talk to him." The apprehension in her voice sends an icy jolt of fear down my spine.

"Be right there." It comes out more steady than I'd ever have thought possible, considering what's going through my head.

Shit. Preston. The kid I tossed into that dumpster. Double shit. Leah's brother!

Oh triple shit! It comes to me in a flash. Leah. With all her preoccupation with anything paranormal, she's an easy target for this demon! I'd been so worried about my family that I'd never given Leah a second thought after she peeled out of here!

"Oh nooo!" I say aloud. I rinse off and my wet body scrambles into my clothes, not even bothering to towel off.

When I get into the living room, Preston is sitting on the sofa next to Margrit. His eyes get wide when he sees me. "You! How'd I know I hadn't seen the last of you?"

He's out of his seat and nose to nose with me. He's a skinny kid with glasses, a few years younger than me. His fists are clenched. He remembers how easily I tossed him into the dumpster, so he's not taking a swing at me. Yet.

"Hold on, man," I say with my palms raised. "You walked into the middle of something—"

"You woulda killed that kid!" he says.

"But I didn't…" I drop my hands. "Because of you."

"Preston…" Margrit called from the sofa. "This is Adam. He wasn't himself that night. He's good, Preston."

"Did I hurt you, man?" I ask. "I'm really sorry I did that."

He looks over to Margrit and takes a deep breath. "Where's my sister, asshole? I know she was coming out here with Jake."

Margrit gets to her feet and steps between us. She puts a hand on his chest. "You need to calm down, Preston. She left here this afternoon." Her eyes are wide. "Now you're saying she never went home?" She shoots a look at me.

I nod at her. "That thing made a threat that both of us would be sorry. I should have known it would go after Leah."

"No. I should have known. I'm getting old and not as sharp as I once was. Damn it!" Her hands shake so bad she clasps them together, sitting on the edge of the seat.

Preston grabs my arm, spinning me around. "What's going on? What is this thing you're talking about? And why's it after Leah?"

Margrit rises and steps closer to Preston. She grabs his hand and answers, "This thing is a demon, Preston. It possessed Adam. I made Leah leave for her own safety."

He jumps away from me like I got the world's biggest case of cooties. "You're possessed?"

"No! I was able to get rid of it!"

Margrit chimes in. "But when Adam vanquished the demon it went after your sister."

I know she's right; that's exactly what must have happened. I'm not proud to admit that part of me is relieved that my sister isn't in danger after all. And then I'm wracked with guilt looking at Preston. He's a skinny, sixteen-year-old kid who's barely holding it together; he's so worried. And from the way he accepts this crazy story, he either has great faith in Margrit, or he's more gifted than I gave him credit for.

Waves of unease flow from Margrit when she looks at me. "It's going to use her the same way it tried to use you. She's not strong enough to resist it like you did, though."

"And with her, there's not going to be any problem getting some guy to comply. This evil spirit doesn't care if it procreates through an ovum or sperm cell. Either way, it wins."

Preston looks horrified as he pulls back staring at each of us in turn. "This thing wants my sister to get pregnant? That's disgusting. Why? And why Leah?"

Margrit takes a deep breath before she answers, "It's not just creating a baby, Preston. This demon will become that baby. This is how it will truly assume a human body. That's its endgame."

"That's sick! No way is my sister getting raped by this thing—a damned demon!" He starts heading out of the room.

Margrit calls out to him. "Wait, we'll go with you! You can't drive in the state you're in. Adam will drive us. We'll find her, Preston."

I'm right on his heels, going out the front door and across the veranda. "Hold up, bud. Margrit can't walk as fast as we can. What about this cop? Jake?" But I curse myself as well. I've got Jake's phone. How am I going to call him?

Margrit yells from behind me, "Take my car. We'll stop at Jake's place and let him know."

He stops at his car and turns back. "Okay."

Margrit hands me the car key and then gets in the passenger seat. When I start the car, she looks over at me. There's no need for words. She's thinking the same thing as me. What if Leah did what I did, leaving town under this entity's control? When I turn my head to watch the drive behind me, wheeling Margrit's vehicle past Preston's car, I reach out and touch Preston's arm.

Like always, his life and history flood into my mind in a split second. Of all Leah's family, he's the closest to her. The one who loves her unconditionally. Funny. It's just like me and my own kid sister. I got Amy, and Leah's got Preston.

I stop the car for a second and grip his arm firmly.

"Hey!" he says, but holds still. He looks at me wide-eyed. He can feel me poking around; nobody's ever been able to sense when I would do that. He tries to pull away, but I grasp tighter. I'm able to reach out to Leah through his…shit—through his love for his sister! Damn, Margrit was right about the power of love.

It comes to me in a flash. She's in town, at a bar. A couple of rough-looking guys hover close by.

This demon thing sure doesn't waste any time. I turn to Margrit. "She's still in Saranac. At some skanky bar."

"Do you know where it is?" she asks.

I let go of Preston's arm. "No." Oh shit, how can we find her?

TWENTY FIVE

I punch it, and we fly down the road heading toward the town. I don't have a clue where to look, but I'm playing my best guess.

After about two minutes Margrit says, "Slow down, Adam." She points to a driveway just up ahead. "That's where Jake lives. Turn in. This demon is not going to relinquish its grip easily. We'll need his help."

Preston puts his hand on the back of my seat, leaning forward. "You really think this demon is in control of her? That's she's possessed?"

I glance into the rearview mirror. "Y'know, you're buying into all this pretty easily, Preston. How come?"

He glances over toward Margrit. "We've all dealt with stuff like this before," he says.

"What? Demons? Possessions?"

"Nope." He leans forward as I lurch off the highway onto Jake's driveway. "Ghosts." He points up at Jake's home. "In that house, actually."

"Why do you think Jake was so receptive to what I told him, Adam?" Margrit chimes in. "He's been down a road like this one before." She snorts. "More than once, actually."

Preston asks, "Yeah, ghosts were one thing, but you guys are saying demons and possession! You think Leah's possessed?"

I ease my foot off the accelerator and turn in toward Jake's house. "Yeah, I do. I just hope we're not too late to shut this thing down." I stop the car behind the police vehicle and leave the engine running. "Stay here. I won't be long."

As I jump out of the car, Jake appears at the front door. "What's going on?" He comes outside, closing the door behind him.

"It's Leah. She never went home. This demon got to her, Jake."

"What? Leah?" His head jerks forward, and his mouth snaps shut when he clues into what's happening. "Oh shit." He looks back to his house. "Sure glad my wife and the girls are on that shopping trip. This is really creepy." He turns back to me. "What do you know?"

"She's in some bar in town. We're gonna need your help getting her out. Maybe arrest her or something till we can help get rid of this thing once and for all." Although I'm not sure how we're going to accomplish that; we have to try.

He thinks for a minute. "She's only seventeen, so she's probably at Tapped Out. Those owners play fast and loose serving minors." He heads back inside. "Let me get my stuff and we'll head over."

I race back to the car as he disappears inside the house. When he comes out again he's in his uniform and strapping on his gun belt. I back out the drive and wait to follow him. "He thinks he knows the bar. Some place called Tapped Out."

Preston groans, "That place is skeevy. I cross the street rather than walk by it. Bikers and lowlifes hang out there. If he's right, we'll sure need a cop to help out."

Jake wastes no time, even using the siren as he races down the road. Margrit's car shudders when I floor the gas pedal to keep up. It's probably never gone this fast before.

"Great. Just great," I say. If he's right and it's a tough bar, this is going to be kind of scary. Not bad enough that we'll be dealing with this demented demon but a bunch of thugs as well? Preston's only sixteen, Margrit's an old lady and me... I'm not exactly Hulk Hogan material, y'know.

Margrit turns to me. "Enough with the negativity. I told you before; you're stronger than you give yourself credit for. You need to firmly believe this, if we're going to help Leah."

She looks back at Preston. "That goes for you, too. Leah loves you more than anyone in this world. Don't underestimate how powerful a weapon love is in saving your sister."

We enter the outskirts of the small town, and Jake turns down a side street. It's dark except for a neon sign that pulses out the message 'Cold Beer'. There are a few Harley's parked on the street out front. Even from inside the car, the beat of heavy metal music throbs through the air.

Jake gets out of the car and waits for us to join him. "Now, listen," he says, "we're not looking for trouble here. We just want to go in and convince Leah to come with us, okay? Let's keep it low-key."

But I know that's probably not going to be the way it goes down. And Jake showing up in uniform is not going to go over well. There's no doubt in my mind that Leah is in there.

I take a deep breath, trying to summon my courage. "I should go in first. There might be a chance that Leah will listen to me."

"No. She's' my sister. She's more likely to listen to me." Preston doesn't wait for an answer but starts going toward the door.

"Hold on!" Jake barks, stopping Preston in his tracks. "First of all you're a minor! You can't go in there without an adult, kid." Jake shoots a hard look at me, "So are you, for that matter. I'll go get her."

Margrit clucks her tongue at us, "It's got to be me. Leah respects me. And as for the hoodlums in-side, no one is going to pick a fight with an old woman. At least let me try."

Shit. She's right. Even Jake knows this. He looks down at his feet for a moment and then looks back at her. "It's worth a shot. But if she won't come out on her own, don't get tangled up arguing the point. Come out and I'll handle it. With any luck she isn't even in that dump."

Margrit shakes her head. "She's in there. I get a very clear sense of her presence." She squeezes Preston's shoulder and then walks into the bar. The last I see of her is the aura of silver before the door closes.

It's awkward as hell standing with Leah's brother and the cop. All three of us feel like tools letting an old woman lead the charge against this hellion. But there's less chance of blood getting spilled with Margrit talking to Leah. And even though the crowd is rough, who would get rough with a woman in her eighties?

After what seems like an hour but is probably more like ten minutes, the old lady comes out. She's visibly shaken, clutching her chest with her hand. "She left with two men. They went out the back door. I tried to get her to come with me, but this isn't Leah we're dealing with. She's not even trying to resist it."

"Come on!" Jake calls over his shoulder, running down the street toward an alleyway to the back.

"Go!" Margrit pushes my shoulder and I take off after him. Preston is just behind me.

We round the corner and come to the back parking lot of the bar. Boxes and trash cans are lined up against the building. Movement in the shadows near the edge of the lot catches my eye and Jake's voice cuts the air.

"Stop right there! Hands where I can see them. Slowly, step away from the girl." He's got his gun pointed at two gorilla-sized guys. Tattooed arms the size of logs stick through leather vests emblazoned with gang colors.

The guy on the left steps forward, a sneer on his sweaty face. "We ain't doin' nuthin' wrong. You got no cause—"

"Leah, get over here."

I hold Preston back when he tries to get by me, on his way over to his sister. Instead, I speak to her. "Leah. I know what happened. I can help you."

Her eyes narrow and when she speaks; even her voice has

changed. It's guttural and raspy. "Help me? You can hardly help yourself. I don't need you anymore." She rubs her hands over herself. "This body will do just as well." She rolls her hips like a stripper, and licking her lips turns to each of the thugs with her. "Don't you think so, boys?"

"Oh my God! Leah!" Preston finally gets it. This girl he's gaping at is no more Leah than I am.

Like a pair of mongrels smelling a bitch in heat, the two guys turn and face off against Jake. One of them cracks his knuckles. "This is a private party, piggy; and you ain't invited."

"That's right, TJ!" Leah eggs him on. "Show me what kind of man you are!"

"I said step away from the girl, NOW!" Jake roars at the two guys. Leveling his gun he barks, "Leave her with us and you're free to go. No questions asked."

The first guy looks over at his partner and then bolts off into the back street. Leah watches him go and snarls. "Coward!" She turns to the other guy and places her hand on his arm. "C'mon, TJ. He won't shoot us. Let's go back to your place and party."

The guy doesn't even glance at Jake. His eyes, glittering with lust wash over her as he wraps his arm around her and starts leading the way to his motorcycle parked nearby.

I look at Jake but he's acting weird. He kind of looks spacey and the hand holding the gun softens. It clatters onto the pavement. Before I have a chance to say anything, Preston bolts over to where Leah is. When she turns, raising her hand like a traffic cop, he comes to a dead stop, even bouncing back like he hit some kind of wall.

Shit! It made Jake's hand release the gun and then swatted Preston away like he was a mosquito. Whatever part of that creature that is Leah, is smothered in the evil of that entity.

She gets on the back of the bike and the TJ guy plunges his foot down on the kick-start. It sputters, but stops. TJ's grin fades as he tries it again, but the same thing happens. He looks down at his bike, gaping puzzlement. "What the hell?"

Margrit brushes by me and comes to a stop next to the

bike. Waves of pure platinum thread through her glowing aura, expanding and growing so dense her body is blurred. She's doing this! Somehow she's managed to stop that bike! "You're not taking her," she says to the guy.

The Leah creature spits at Margrit and then gets off the bike.''That was a cheap trick, old woman. But you can't hold me here."

The biker dude just stares at Margrit like she's some kind of witch and then he joins Leah, stepping closer to Margrit.

My ears start ringing, and a wave of… I don't know... certitude or something flows over me. I leap in front of them, shielding Margrit with my body. "Astaroth! I command you to leave this girl!" Astaroth? Where did that name come from? But I don't get a chance to think about it watching Leah.

It has an effect! The sneer on her face is replaced with wide-eyed shock. Even a trace of fear comes through in a fleeting second before the demon recovers.

"So, you know my name?" It sneers. "Big deal. You and this old hag can't stop me. Me and my new boyfriend are out of here. You'll never find me, so don't bother trying."

It's bluffing. I can tell by the way, Leah's hand closes on Biker Guy's' arm pulling him back.

"Leah? You have to fight this thing! Don't let it control you anymore." Preston is openly crying, again racing forward to grab his sister. "For Christ's sake! Leah! I love you! Fight this beast! I love you Leeeeeahhhh!"

The last comes out as a shrieking wail that goes right through my heart. And it's somehow pierced through the possession that has Leah imprisoned. The dark, smoky aura of the entity lightens and there's an earthy tone that's pure Leah.

She turns to look at Preston, the hardness in her eyes gone, replaced with confusion. This thing hijacked her so fast she wasn't even aware of why she was here.

Margrit joins Preston. "Leah. You're a good person. I love you too. I love that you're kind and generous. You won't even hurt an insect, let alone your brother. He needs you and loves you."

The demon's power is shrinking. Margrit and I both see that. Even Jake is able to emerge from whatever fugue state the thing put him in, grabbing his gun from the ground. He fires a shot in the air, then levels the pistol at TJ. "Next three are going right into you, buster."

The blast breaks the moment, and Leah's face once more becomes a mask, her eyes narrow with contempt.

TJ looks at Jake, and without another word turns and runs down the alleyway.

There's only the demon left, staring us down.

TWENTY SIX

Ohhh, Jake! My hero!" the Leah-thing says. It's trying to coo, but there's a guttural sound in its voice, like phlegm. I'm disgusted and look over at Jake.

His eyes are riveted on her as she steps slowly toward him. "You're sooo strong! Sooo brave," she says, her voice now a smoky whisper. She won't take her eyes off him. I can practically hear the message she's projecting, feeling her evil power ensnaring him. It reminds me of what it did to me the first time I encountered this demon. Of course she'd target him. Of the three of us, he'd be the most malleable to her will. Margrit's an old woman, Preston's Leah's brother, and I already rejected Astaroth.

Margrit takes my hand in hers and then barks out an order, staring hard at the Leah-thing. "Stop! You will leave this girl, NOW!"

I feel the surge of power vibrating in my chest from the old woman. For a moment I'm hopeful that it will be enough. Enough to stop this hateful spirit for good.

It pauses briefly before dismissing us and continues moving. And whatever it's doing is working! Jake's hand shakes and then falls to his side. Leah's finger trails over his cheek and she smiles. "Good boy. I'll have to make do with you. Leah always thought you were attractive, so there is that. You'll father my child." Her eyes are dangerous slits when she turns to us. "But first you must kill them."

His hand lifts and now the gun is aimed squarely at Margrit! There's a blank look in his eyes, totally under the demon's influence!

"Wait! Astaroth. You wanted me, remember?" I step in front of Margrit and push Preston out of the line of fire. "I can give you what you want! A child with my gifts! Think of it! I'll go with you. But you must leave these people alone!" My heart races and my body quakes as I do this, knowing she's just as likely to kill me out of revenge. Hell hath no fury like a demon scorned.

Oh my God! My life flashes before me as I wait for her to speak. Time crawls like a slug, each memory from being a toddler skinning my knee, my time with Nana, Amy learning my name and giggling every time I played peekaboo... Frames of my life play in my mind right up to the present moment. It could all end in a heartbeat.

"No, Adam. No. Don't do this." Margrit's voice sounds like it's coming from under water, vague and inconsequential.

This is something I have to do! No more deaths at this thing's hands! Especially Margrit and Leah's brother. I brought this beast here, and now it's up to me to face the consequences.

Leah's hand closes over Jake's and his arm lowers. She looks at me and glances back to Jake. "I don't knowww…" she says, her voice a rasp. She's smiling slyly; I can see it's really me Astaroth wants.

"How can I convince you?" I say.

She tilts her head. "Beg me for favor."

I drop to my knees, clasping my hands before me. "Let them go. We'll run away together and create this child." When the Leah demon smiles, I add the coup de grace. "You were right and I was wrong. I was a fool to let Leah leave today.

She's perfect for this. Your power will be unstoppable!"

"No way!" Preston darts out from behind me. "Leah! Please don't do it! You can't mate with this thing. Adam doesn't know what he's talking about!"

He takes a step but then is forced to the ground, folding like a jackknife. This time, however, he howls with pain, and there's a rivulet of blood seeping out of his nose.

I make no move to join Margrit when she kneels at Preston's side, trying to help him. Instead I rise and walk over to the Leah-thing.

Oh man, it's taken her over something fierce! A rank smell—like an overflowing sewer is emanating from every pore that's so strong my eyes water. I swallow back the instinctive retch in my throat and smile down at her. "Let's go. If you hurt any of them again, I won't do this. You may like pain and suffering but I don't." I pause for effect and grin. "Not yet, anyway." From the corner of my eye, I see Jake step over to help Margrit with the boy. I push down any sense of relief that this thing is actually letting them go. I must guard my thoughts around this thing.

Leah's fingers curl over the back of my neck and she pulls me closer. "You have a lot to learn, Adam. You'll grow to love ultimate power. The suffering of the weak is just an added spice to savor."

Her lips brush mine, and I have to quickly erase the flash of squirming worms from my mind. This thing is capable of seeing my thoughts, and I must be very, very careful. But in that faint touch, I also felt Leah. There's still a part of her soul in there, cowering and confused as to what's happening. Like a kid trapped in a dark closet, I can feel the real Leah whimper.

I pull back a little and take the thing's hand in mine. "Let's go. I can't wait to get started." Anything to make sure the others will be safe. I'll figure it out as I go.

She pauses, bringing me to a halt. "Just one teensy-weensy thing more." At her scathing look, Margrit is pushed to the ground. The clunk of her head hitting the pavement reverberates through me like a knife hitting bone.

When I look, there's no sign of Margrit's essence. There's nothing there except Jake and now Preston scrambling to her. It's all I can do not to run over as well, but instead I shrug. "Ready to go?" I say instead.

She tugs my arm and we're off, racing down the back street, destined for who knows where.

TWENTY SEVEN

"WAIT!" I gasp for breath, my heart pounding like a jackhammer, coming to a stop. We've been running for five minutes straight and this demon thing in Leah's body shows no sign of wear. I have no idea where Leah-thing is leading us.

"It's not that much farther. Come on!" She pulls at my arm but I wave her off. The pink sundress is damp with her sweat, clinging to her thighs. This is the only thing about her that shows any sign of exertion. She's not even chilled by the night air on her bare arms and shoulders.

"Where are you taking me?" I can barely get the words out, bent over and gulping air. My thighs and lungs scream with pain from the race through town.

"You seriously need to work out more, Adam. For a young guy you're in pretty poor physical condition." Her fingers scrape through her hair, pulling it up off her shoulders. She stretches her head from one side to the other, easing her muscles, a big grin on her face. "Now this is why I love this body. What's not to love about a seventeen-year-old girl who exercises and eats organic?"

When I straighten, I feel Jake's cell phone in the back

pocket of my jeans. It's just a fleeting thought; cell phones leave an electronic trail. I hardly dare to dwell on that realization, not with this thing's capability to read me.

My hand drifts along the Leah-thing's neck, and I contort my face into a leer, gazing down at her body. "How much farther? Now that I've agreed to do this, I want to get on with it. Where are we going?"

Leah's chin lifts higher, and there's triumph in her eyes looking over at me. From just that faint touch of her skin, I get a clear sense of its cocky self-confidence.

"Nowhere special. Not yet. There's a motel nearby where we'll hole up for a few days, hiding in plain sight." Absently, she twirls a lock of hair in her fingers, trying to look cute and flirty.

There's no sense in reminding her of the bodies she left in her wake back in Watertown—not if I'm going to pull this off. Although I have no idea if that's even possible. That cell phone... hmmm.

"Let's go, then!" I look around trying to get a sense of where I am—a street sign, anything. The area is dimly lit with only a corner store and a gas station. It's mostly small houses with the odd vacant lot. Hard to believe there would be a motel out this way, when there's nothing special or touristy about it.

"My my my... You've certainly warmed up to my idea. In some ways taking over Leah, directing her is so much easier. Fighting you and then with that old hag interfering... it was getting soooo tiresome." She takes the lead, glancing back over her shoulder in a pose that is supposed to be sexy.

I won't deny it—it was alluring. She jutted a hip and arched her back, her cotton dress clinging to every curve and valley.

I curse my own weakness, but smile. "Yeah. It was kind of wearing me out too. I'm glad you decided to give me another chance. I mean my genes have got to be better than some biker guy." My tone and words are so saccharin sweet, it makes my teeth ache, but this thing is a glutton for compliments.

"Exactly! And Leah is so easy to manipulate. My plan

works better this way, even if I miss out on living your experience when we actually get down to screwing. Especially since it's your official first time. Heavy petting doesn't count in this game."

The vulgar term coming out of Leah's mouth makes it even more obscene. Which brings up another fear. I'm not sure I can go through with this when the moment of truth comes around. What will this demon do if I can't? Performance anxiety might turn into a certain death sentence.

I manage a small laugh. "The two of us being virgins... that makes it more perfect for you doesn't it?" Got to keep it preoccupied in its gloating. "Hang on a minute. My shoelace is undone." I bend quickly and make a show of tying it. When I straighten, my hand slips into my back pocket, and I click a button on the side of the phone.

These cell phones have hidden programming to pick up on conversations. I know that's real having experienced a plethora of ads for sunglasses when I mentioned sunglasses in a conversation. If I can say a street name, maybe I'll leave an electronic trail for Jake to pick up on. Surely, he's savvy enough to link his phone to his laptop.

The demon doesn't seem to notice what I'm doing when it continues blathering its own praises. "Virgins! Well obviously that was the way to go! I know this gig's been done before by another, whose name I won't mention. Just thinking about Him makes me wanna puke. But the irony is compelling, no?"

"Fer shure! But how are we going to pay for a motel room? I'm tapped out, unless—"

"Not to worry! I've got this! From now on, we'll have whatever luxury we could ever wish for."

Finally, a street sign shows. I've been looking high and low since we came down this road. "Merrivale Motel! That's ironic too. Merry Valley? Sounds good to me! Get it?" It's weak, but I managed to get the road's name out there without looking too suspicious. I hope.

"Don't give up the day job, Adam. There's no chance for you in stand-up. I just hope you're more entertaining in bed."

She shoots another suggestive smile at me, as she rubs her stomach below her belly button.

Watching her, I'm both turned on and repulsed. Yuck.

But I grin like a fool at her. "They say practice makes perfect. I'm all about getting in all the practice I can."

"That's what I want! See? This is much more fun than resisting me, Adam. I knew you'd eventually see it my way." The smug look on its face is anything but pretty.

I keep trying to engage it in conversation as a deeper part of my brain tries to figure out a plan. "So you've tried this before, haven't you? But this time you're sure it will work?"

She rolls her eyes and then points to a lighted sign a short walk away. "Yes. I picked the wrong targets, time and time again. Always some simple girl who ended up killing herself rather than carry my child."

"So, how's this any different?" Poor Leah. She'd hate me saying that.

"The times, they are a changing." After it giggles like a hyena, it continues, "No one here would sacrifice themselves like that. It's a me/me time you live in Adam." She waves her hand. "No, having a child outside of marriage is no longer as big a deal as it once was."

I nod. Anything to keep it talking.

It pauses before going across the road to the motel. "Whatever is left of Leah in this body will never end her life when she realizes what's happening. And if you start getting cold feet, you know what will happen to your friends."

I snort. "Friends? I thought the old lady could help me defeat you. She was a fraud. I'd rather back the winning team."

"Exactly my point! Now you can stay here while I get our room squared away or watch and learn."

"If it's all the same to you, I'd like to learn at the hands of a master, not that charlatan old woman."

Her finger rises and drifts along the line of my jaw. "You're showing more and more promise, Adam."

TWENTY EIGHT

The clerk at the desk looks up from his cell phone when we enter the motel's office. He does a double-take, eyeing Leah and then glancing over at me with narrow eyes. "Need to see some ID. And a credit card to rent a room. How old is she?"

The Leah-thing steps forward, and immediately the suspicion on the guy's face fades. "We'd like a room, preferably an end unit. You don't need anything more from us. Understood?"

When he nods, his double chin quivers while a bead of sweat trickles down his temple. "Shu... sure. Room twenty is free." The bored attitude has been replaced with a blank acceptance. Even his aura, which was a pale green when we came in, dissolves into a charcoal gray similar to the one surrounding Leah.

Leah raps the countertop. "Give me the key card then." When he scuttles over to the drawer to get it, she continues, "If anyone asks about a young woman and dark-haired guy coming in tonight, you've never seen anything. Got it?"

He nods once more and slides the card across the counter.

But her hand closes on his and her nails bite into his skin so hard that he yelps.

"I got it!"

"Good. We may be here for a couple of days. See that we aren't disturbed." She snaps the key card up and then adds in a singsong voice that makes a shudder skitter through me. "Except for breakfast. You may bring that at ten tomorrow morning. Denny's Grand Slam and lots of OJ."

She gestures with her finger for me to follow her. "I love orange juice. Coffee is so overrated. It's great being human and actually having taste buds."

As I follow her from the office and down the long outside walkway to the end unit, she starts to sing, even pinching the hem of her dress and twirling. "Girls just wanna have fu-un. Oh yeah, girls just wanna have fun!" Waves of pleasure and anticipation waft from her like a bad smell.

I swallow hard knowing time is running out. I'll soon be stuck in that room with this demon. I'm running out of options. I'm literally sweating bullets when she stops and slides the key card through the reader, all the while eyeing me suggestively.

'You can do this Adam. Believe. Have faith'. Margrit's words surprise me when they bubble up from my memory. My shoulders pull back, which the Leah-thing immediately misinterprets, glancing down at my lower body and licking her lips. Ugh.

When she opens the door, a waft of pine-scented cleaner masking the musty body odor of previous occupants drifts into my nostrils. A dresser with cigarette burn marks sits across from a sagging double bed, cheerfully covered in some kind of geometric print. I cross the room to peek out of the heavy curtains to the back, but everything outside is black as tar.

At the click of the door closing a feeling of claustrophobia threatens, now that I'm trapped here with this thing. She saunters over, snuggling close, her hands slithering over my back until they lower cupping my butt. It would be a nineteen-year-old guy's dream come true if not for the creature inhabiting this young woman.

My hands feel like lead as I drag them up to rest on her hips.

"Mmmm... I can't decide which is better. Being inside a guy's body or a girl's, anticipating and getting warmed up." She rises on her tiptoes and her tongue rolls over my earlobe, before nipping it with sharp teeth. She's even grinding her pelvis against me.

'Believe.' I take a deep breath and let it out slowly, even hitching it to feign arousal. My hand skitters up the curve of her waist and then higher until it rests on her breast, over her heart. It's not the plush softness under my hand that I'm concentrating on, though.

Lean gutturally moans and tugs the elastic smocking covering her chest lower. Now it's flesh meeting flesh, a fact I try not to dwell on.

'Leah.' I focus on the spitfire I've just met—annoying as hell but well meaning. *'Leah'*. A flash of her fills my mind, frightened, glancing over her shoulder as she runs away. It's the same expression, the same girl who was in my dream. I'd foretold this moment when the demon would threaten her. And now it has conquered.

The Leah-thing pulls back, its face now revealing its ugly essence contorting Leah's mouth into a snarl. "Stop it! Whatever you're doing, just stop it!"

But I pull it closer with my other hand, still feeling Leah's heartbeat under my palm. My mind is filled with another scene that makes my breath hitch. Leah as a middle-aged woman, her eyes full of affection staring back at me, taking my hand as we walk along a shoreline. My love for her brings tears to my eyes.

It's us!

Oh my God. It's our future that I'm seeing.

And somehow that vision strengthens the first impression of her spirit, her soul inside this body. Hope replaces fear, and she even manages a slight smile.

All the while, the demon hisses, twisting in my arms to be free. "You fool! It's meeeeee you need, not the simpering wannabe that Leah is! She'll never be anything!"

My grip tightens, holding on to the vision of Leah with everything I've got! I cry out aloud, "Leah! Come to me! You can do this! I need you to do this. We've got a future together!" Any qualm I might have had about letting Leah know how I was drawn to her earlier, vanishes in the moment. Honesty and love are all I've got to save her! "We love each other, Leah."

For a moment the demon shrinks and its movements falter. I can hear Leah in my mind.

"Adam! Help meee!"

The desperation in her voice is an arrow to my heart. The words pour out of me, stronger this time, "We love each other, Leah! We will marry and have children! You have to trust me when I tell you that!"

Tears fill my eyes when I see into this body, a body that one day I will cherish as I do my own. Leah is expanding, getting stronger, starting to reclaim what is hers.

We SEE each other. We are one! Bonds of trust and love tie us, making us stronger.

"ADAM! Stop this! You'll be sorrrrry!" But the demon's voice is slurred and fainter than its earlier screams.

'Believe, Trust yourself, Adam.' Again Margrit's words bubble up, A vibration that begins in my solar plexus expands, getting faster and harder. And it's holding the real Leah deep inside, infusing her with energy.

What comes out of this thing's mouth isn't the Leah I love. It's a harsh growl."*You'll never beat me, Adam! I'll kill you and this wretched girl! There's always another body that I can claim. I don't need you.*"

It hits me then. In this last claim, the demon isn't lying. Even if Leah and I manage to banish it from her being, it will prey on someone else.

No. This time it has to die.

It's fighting tooth and nail, its claws trying to tear at my face. I grab its wrists and stare into eyes of pure hate. Leah is in the background a shimmering soul that's coming forward, inch by steady inch.

"Leah! Stop! We can't push this beast from you. Hang on to it just as hard as I'm holding these wrists. Between us, we can trap this monster. It can't be free to infect anyone else."

Her voice sounding in my mind is pure fear. *"I can't go on like this. It's hurting meeee! I can't breathe!"* As if to underscore this, her nose begins to bleed, two thick red lines roll over her lips and fall from her chin.

Oh my God. It's killing her from the inside!

'Fear, anger, hate. Love is stronger and multidimensional.' Again Margrit's words resonate in my mind.

"You've got to be strong, Leah! Don't be scared. We will beat this creature!" Even as I cry these words, I'm struggling to avoid the thing's feet trying to kick me away. When its knee rises catching me between the legs, sheer agony threatens to fold me like a flap of paper.

"NO!" Its scream is far away and barely registers.

Stars float in the periphery of my vision and then everything gets kind of blurry. My grip on her wrists slips.

"Astaroth! By the power of light and love I command you to stop!"

I shake my head barely able to comprehend how Margrit's voice just got louder in my head. I feel a strong grip cover my hands holding Leah's wrists and a body presses against mine.

When my eyes open, I can hardly believe what's happened!

Jake is beside me holding Leah's arms high and he's covered her thrashing legs with one of his.

Holy Mother of God! Margrit! She's here. Rubbing ashes across Leah's forehead. Hell! Even Preston is here.

Preston's fingers stroke Leah's cheek and he murmurs a litany of love. "Be strong, Leah. You can do this. You have to do this because I can't lose you. I love you too much!"

When Margrit turns to me, there's a goose egg on the side of her head but other than that she's okay. "Help me, Adam! Call to her! She needs to feel the love you have for her."

"But what about this demon? We need to destroy it, Margrit."

"I've got this!" She faces the demon. It recoils and curses

her in a language that's foreign and guttural, but there's understanding in Margrit's soul.

The moment slows like honey, and the demon's darkness clears, showing its true face. Eyes that burn like embers below a thick and hoary brow, curled horns of a goat protruding just above. Blood and gore pour over razor teeth in a gaping mouth.

"Adam!" Margrit's voice yanks me from the shocking horror of its visage.

I look past it and Leah is there. Her aura expands, crowding the demon thing with tendrils of earthy brown. Her gray eyes focus, and when we gaze at each other, words are a pale tribute to the love we have for each other. The pureness of her soul, her kindness and innocence capture me in a magnetic pull so strong that I lose myself in her being. We are one, even as Preston's love surrounds her.

Margrit's harsh words to the demon are a background noise when I meld with Leah. Jake's grunts as he struggles against the demon's last thrusts are whispers in the wind.

The peace and surety of us—Leah and me—are the pure essence of love. I would have died to protect her from this demon, and I know she would have made the same sacrifice for me. We're in a never-ending circle—no, a sphere that swirls over us and through us. There is only love! I could stay in this state forever.

I don't know how long we drift like this. It could be moments or centuries. Time is a concept that no longer exists, gazing into Leah's soul.

I feel something touch my shoulder but I shrug it away. I don't want to leave this space, but Margrit's voice breaks through.

"Adam! Come back! Leah! Come back to us!"

The palms of my hand against Leah's falls away and my fingers try to grasp hers but falter. I feel and see us separate, and a powerful sense of loss hits me so hard that I fall to my knees. When I come to, she's in front of me, also on the floor.

"Is that it?" Jake's voice is harsh bringing my focus and

reality back like a slap in the face. He continues as I stare at Leah. "Is this damned thing finally gone?"

Preston lowers and he pulls his sister into his arms. "Leah. Oh my God. I thought I'd lost you forever." When he eases back he takes a tissue from his pocket to clear the blood from her face. His voice is a soft moan. "Oh God, it hurt youuuu!"

"I'm okay." Leah murmurs, tugging her dress higher.

Margrit steps over to where I am, and her hand rests on my shoulder as she answers Jake. "The damned thing is finished, not just beaten. It will be a long time before this beast leaves the depths of hell, if ever."

The relief soaring through me is intoxicating. I can't stop the quip, "You mean like when hell freezes over?"

She cuffs my head, but then leans over to plant a kiss on my hairline. "I believed in you, Adam. And more importantly, you believed in yourself."

It's true. After another moment savoring this wonderful truth, I look over at Leah. She's enough in the moment, feeling embarrassed about her dress that she's even blushing. It's so sweet and innocent that I want to leap over and kiss her.

But I don't.

She looks shyly at me. "All those things that you said..."

"They were the truth, Leah. We experienced the future—our future. That's how I knew we could defeat this thing. We have to be together. It's destiny." I shift closer and even cup her cheek in my hand. "But this is now. We haven't had a chance to know each other to actually feel love. We sort of borrowed... from all our tomorrows."

She swallows hard, looking down and then her chin lifts. "It was amazing. But—"

Margrit places her other arm over Leah's shoulder. "Neither one of you are ready yet. Marriage is a ways down the road for you two."

Jake who'd been standing watching, still shell-shocked a bit from all this supernatural stuff, now bellows, "Marriage? What the hell? We fight this demon thing and you bring up marriage. Not to mention she's only seventeen!"

Leah grins up at him. “And still a virgin!” She sneaks a quick peek at me. “I am, right? I mean—”

“Yup!” My hands pull back and fly high between us. “Not guilty! Although...”

Margrit slaps my hands, “Enough! You both have a lot of growing up to do!”

I look over at the three of them in turn. This could have gone so badly if they hadn’t shown up when they did. “How’d you find us?”

TWENTY NINE

Preston, with a big grin on his face is the first to speak. "Margrit, of course. Although I was picking up snippets of a seedy motel."

I look at Jake and then pull his cell phone from my back pocket. "I tried to leave clues on this thing. You may have some odd charges on your bill. I wasn't sure what button I clicked but I had to try something."

"I'll let you know, kid, if you pocket dialed Taiwan. I'm not sure the department will cover that."

I look at Margrit when I pull myself up from the floor. "Are you okay? I seriously thought you were a goner when I heard your head bang on the pavement. Your, you know..." I glance at Jake knowing this is all more mumbo-jumbo for him to hear, but continue anyway, "your aura was nowhere to be seen."

She chuckles, and her hand rubs at the bump on her head. "I was out cold. Jake was about to go into that seedy bar to call an ambulance when I came to."

Preston jumps in. "It was actually only a few minutes that she was out. But it scared the heck outta us! Especially when that thing had Leah in its grip, and you seemed to be going along with it."

Margrit slumps onto the bed staring at me. "I knew you weren't. But I was worried that you wouldn't be able to keep that secret from the creature. How did you manage to hide your intentions?"

I sit next to her, and it's like we're back at the stump, sitting together. "You told me that evil is self-absorbed. I used flattery like crazy to hide my true thoughts deep in my mind. It's like I had two conscious parts, keeping a lock on the true ones that it couldn't enter."

Her head tips to the side as she gazes at me. "I didn't teach you how to do that."

I snort. "I'm a guy, Margrit. A hormonal nineteen-year-old guy! Think about it! I see a pretty girl and well you know what could happen to my body. I have to have another section in my brain to take over and well... keep things under control, if you know what I mean."

Leah pierces me with a glare and fairly spits the words, "What girl? Are you ogling every girl and getting... well, you know?"

Oh my God! She's staking a claim on me, and I don't even know her last name! But still, her jealousy warms me.

Jake comes to the rescue. "He doesn't live in a vacuum, Leah. I'm sure he looked at you the same way when you met."

Preston stands up quickly, peering down at me, "Not my sister, buddy. You better not be—"

"Hey! Everyone take a chill pill, okay! We just battled a freakin' demon, and now you're getting all self-righteous about my nonexistent sex life?" Sheesh! Give a guy a break! "Can we go now? This place makes me want to take a shower."

Leah stands up and grumbles. "You want to take a shower? What about me? I had that dirty stinkin' demon inside me! I'm going to have to soak in a hot tub for a month to feel clean again!"

Preston goes over and hugs her as they walk out of the room. "Even though I know you're totally clean, we'll do a smudging over you when we get home." When she gawks at him he adds, "Out in the backyard, out of Mom's sight, okay?"

I help Margrit to her feet, and she holds my arm as we leave the room. She chuckles and whispers, leaning in closer. "Sure you and Leah are destined to get together? She's nice but... well, she can be bullheaded too."

I can't help but smile. "I don't understand it either, Margrit. But I saw us in the future. We were so happy and still so much in love even though we were old, man! I mean she was gorgeous! At forty!"

"That old, huh?" Jake guffaws from behind us, closing the door to the room. "Careful kid, I'm hitting the big four-oh, next year."

Margrit pats my arm. "You'll stay the night at my home. Even though the danger is past, Preston has a point. I'm going to smudge the hell out of both of us!"

When we get to Jake's car, I pile in next to Leah in the backseat while Margrit rides shotgun. Sitting next to Leah, all I can think about is how wonderful it felt when we connected, borrowing from the future. From the warmth of her thigh so close to mine, to the way her body, her energy flow eases, drifting into mine, tentative at first. I know she's thinking the same thing.

It's both thrilling and scary knowing our destiny yet we're still practically strangers. The attraction on both sides is a presence that folds us both in its arms.

Jake breaks the spell.

"I spoke with Detective Cooke in Watertown. He and his partner will be here around ten tomorrow morning."

I meet his eyes in the rearview mirror before he pulls out of the parking lot onto the street.

"I'll be at Margrit's." I sigh, sinking lower into the seat. This isn't over yet. There's still the dead bodies left in Watertown to account for before I'm able to go home to see my family. It's a surprise, a pleasant surprise, when Leah's hand slips over mine and she gives it a squeeze.

"It'll be okay, Adam."

My heart flips and I grasp her tight. For a moment the trace of what we felt when we connected fighting the demon is there. It's all kind of mixed up with Leah's spirit, how kind and wonderful she is. It's all I can do to stop myself from leaning closer and kissing her cheek but the timing is definitely off. Plus there's her protective brother and Margrit. Jake might even deck me.

"Thanks, Leah." I give her fingers a final squeeze and remove my hand from hers. Again, the sense of loss leaving her touch makes me feel kind of hollow. But that's how it goes... for now.

When Jake parks in front of the skanky bar for us to get Margrit's car, he frowns looking at the windshield of her car. "A ticket? Who the hell gave you a ticket at this time of night and here of all places?"

He stops the car and walks over to Margrit's gray jalopy. Snatching the pink slip from the windshield, he rolls his eyes. "I'll take care of this."

When I help her into her side of the car, I pause for a moment. "Think we should go in for a nightcap, Margrit?"

The horror in her eyes is quickly replaced by a smile when she sees me smirk. "You! Just drive me home, will you? I'm tired."

I round the front of the car and see Leah roll down the window, waving to stop me. "Hey! Don't leave town before I get a chance to say goodbye."

Stepping over, I lean into the window, "This could be goodbye, right here, right now. But maybe more a 'so long for now' or 'see ya later.' We'll see each other again. There's that destiny thing going on, you know."

Her hand bunches in my T-shirt, and she tugs me closer. "Even so, I want to see you again before you go. I'll be at Margrit's first thing in the morning, for a proper goodbye."

I grin but manage to hold the smart-ass retort to myself. We're not even married, not even a couple, and I'm getting henpecked. It's adorable. Before I even know it, I lean in and kiss the tip of her nose. "Lookin' forward to it, Leah."

Jake turns and glares at us. "All right. Enough with the

kissy-face stuff. I got to get home at some point tonight. Claire and the girls are due back anytime."

I can take the hint. I ease back and then join Margrit in the car. As we drive from the town I have to ask, "Did you know that Leah and I will someday be together? You're able to sense things better than me but still..."

She nods. "Yes, when I first saw you two together I could see the connection. You both are old souls who've shared other lifetimes. Both of your auras became richer when you were together, even if yours was clouded by that demon."

"So when will this happen?" Funny. I'm looking forward to it, being with Leah. Even funnier that it isn't the sex drive taking charge with this feeling. Okay! But not *just* the sex drive, all right?

"I can't tell you that. I mean I could but I'm not going to. You both must walk your own path and grow before you're ready for that."

I chuckle. "Not even a hint? C'mon! I helped shoot this demon to hell, it's the least you can do! And look what I went through when it was inside me! You're not being fair, Margrit." Part of me is teasing and part is deadly serious.

"Let's just say, I'll be around to dance at your wedding."

And that was all she'd say, ending with a mysterious smile.

THIRTY

True to her word, Leah pulls into the driveway at just after eight this morning. Considering all we'd been through the night before I was relieved that it wasn't at the crack of dawn. I stand on the veranda sipping a coffee, watching her come up the walkway. Her hair is loose, flowing over her shoulders while the sun's rays paint threads of gold through it.

She smiles up at me, and I can see that she's even taken time to put lipstick on and darken her eyelashes. She totally doesn't need makeup, but I am flattered that she's taken the trouble to impress me even more.

In the bright light of the day, her gray eyes are flecked with blue when she looks up at me. "Good morning! How did you sleep?"

"Great! Margrit's sofa isn't the most comfortable but after the nights I spent with that demon hovering... I don't want to talk about that, though." A snippet of her walking along the shore, looking at me in that dream I'd had flits in my head. "You want to walk with me to the lake?"

"Sure. I'll just say hi to Margrit and we'll go." With that she goes into the house, and the sounds of her voice and Margrit's drift out. In another moment she is back.

I set the mug of coffee down and then take her hand walking down the steps. Even though the image of her mother chewing her out about missing church, traipsing out to see that old gypsy, flashes in my head from the brief touch, I don't comment on it. If her mother knew what Leah had been through the night before… the woman would have a stroke.

"So, you're going back to Buffalo? I mean after you finish with the detectives?" She watches her step as we cross the yard but glances up at me when she finishes speaking.

I don't need to be a mind reader to know that she is going to miss me. Not from the look in her eyes. "Yeah. When I left home almost a year ago, it wasn't on the best of terms. I need to settle things with my parents and my older brother. Not to mention that I miss my little sister Amy like crazy. You'd like her." I stop and take a breath. "No. You're going to *love* her!"

She smiles, and taking my hand, resumes walking. "I'm looking forward to meeting all of your family." Immediately her face colors a pretty pink. I can feel the sudden shyness flood through her, recalling my words the night before—that we are destined to be together, married at some future point in time. "I mean in time, you know. Not right away."

I stop dead in my tracks and pull her around to face me. "Leah. I really want to get to know you. I mean I already know lots of things about you, things that I pick up from just the touch of your hand. I guess what would be more accurate, is that I want to *experience* you."

When her eyes went wide and she pulled back, I added quickly, "Do stuff together. Be surprised, enchanted, laugh, and even get angry with you." When she falls into step beside me, it feels so normal and right.

"What are you going to do with your life, Adam? You said you worked with some private detective. Are you going to do that again?"

"Funny you should ask that. It was actually the first job I ever had that I liked. And my gifts, sensing things about people and objects comes in mighty handy. I might do that. But first I want to finish high school. Who knows, I may even join the police force." The idea that had been niggling at the back of my brain took shape in that moment.

"That could be cool."

We emerge from the forest and I gaze at the water a few moments, inhaling the fresh air and the warmth of the sun. I turn to her. "What about you? What are you going to do with your life? I mean aside from marrying me, which in itself would be awesome?"

She slaps my arm playfully. "Is that a proposal? Aren't you supposed to get down on your knees?"

When I smile, she continues, "I'm going to go to college and either become a teacher or go into social work. I'll figure out which once I'm there. In another year."

"As long as college isn't in Europe or halfway across the country, I'm fine with that. Say that you're going to stay in New York. Please." But I already know she is thinking of Syracuse University. Still, it would be nice to hear it.

"It matters to you? Does that mean you'll come and visit me?" She shifts from side to side, her smile tentative looking up and meeting my gaze.

Damn, but she's pretty! "Wild horses couldn't keep me away! I meant it when I said I want to do stuff together."

That is just the answer she wants to hear. It isn't just her feet skipping along the pebbled beach, her heart is doing a light cartwheel. And in that moment, watching her, totally at one with the water, the earth and the sky is exactly like my dream. Except for the dark shadow that had clouded me, making her frightened, is gone now.

Now, it's just us... and it's perfect.

***

An hour later, walking back through the forest, we're both silent. This taste of a relationship forming will soon be hijacked for a time, replaced with the harsh reality of a police interrogation. Jake is hopeful, but still, what if I say the wrong thing? My mouth has gotten me into trouble enough in the past, that it's a real concern now.

The Watertown police car is parked in Margrit's driveway and two detectives, their butts propped up against the hood of the car wait. This is it. Leah squeezes my hand and murmurs that it will all work out.

The two men in plain clothes walk toward us. The older, shorter one speaks first, "Adam Rafferty? I'm Detective Cooke, and this is Detective Spearman. We're here to—"

But I don't hear the rest of it when I see Mike's caddy pull into the driveway behind the police car. He's a far cry from the cavalry, but it still makes my heart leap in my chest. At least it's a friend, someone who was once a cop who'll give me some moral support.

I straighten and pause letting the detectives continue coming over to speak to me. "Yes. I'm Adam Rafferty. Sorry I kept you waiting." When the second car door slams I look past them and see the guy from my first case! The lawyer, Mr. Wilson, is coming along with Mike!

Oh my God! Mike's brought the lawyer we had investigated in Watertown! Now *that's* the cavalry!

The lawyer calls out as he walks over. "I'm Mr. Rafferty's attorney, Anthony Wilson. You won't mind if I sit in when you question him."

It's not a request but rather a statement. Mike grins and walks over to shake Margrit's hand. She's come down from the veranda, watching all of this silently. "I'm Mike Drogan, Adam's friend."

She takes his hand, but at this distance I can't hear her reply.

The lawyer takes charge immediately. "Adam will ride with us. We can follow you back to Watertown, or if you'd prefer, we'll meet at the local police station for the questioning."

"No. We'd prefer going back to home turf. Just follow us. Let's get this show underway. We've waited more than a few days to question your client." Detective Cooke taps his taller partner and starts going back to his vehicle.

"Hey! Can I have a minute to say goodbye to Mrs. Kovacs? And my girlfriend?" It's out before I even know it.

I watch Mike step over and chat with the two detectives as Leah and I go over to Margrit. She's actually got tears in her eyes when she looks up at me, her voice hitching. "You take care, Adam. But don't be a stranger."

I hug her and feel her fragility. She's like a little bird in my arms. Hard to believe the power she had last night fighting the demon. "Margrit. I don't know how to thank you for all the help you gave me."

"Just be safe. That's a good start." She eases back and looks up into my eyes, "You never did finish painting my house, you know. When this mess is over, come back for a few days. It'd be nice to see you and just *be*. No demon to fight. Just a good visit to catch up."

I grin and nod my head not trusting myself to speak; the tears are just behind my eyes and my throat is tight.

Leah steps in when Margrit releases me. She actually hugs me tight and then slips a piece of paper into my hand. "It's my phone number and email addy. I want to know how this goes down. Promise me you'll call."

I kiss her forehead and then give her a tight hug, deeply inhaling the clean, sweet scent of her skin and her hair. "I will." And she surprises me with a kiss on the lips. A tender touch of her lips on mine.

"Okay, Adam. We'd better hit the road now." Mike shakes Margrit's hand again and then Leah's. "Nice meeting you both. I'm glad Adam had you to turn to."

When we get in Mike's car and are driving behind the police, Mike catches my eye from the rearview mirror beside him. "So... what's with the girl? She's a little out of your league, Adam. Punchin' above your weight again, I see."

I shake my head but smile. If he only knew, he'd just met my future wife.

THIRTY ONE

Three months later...

"I still don't understand why you won't go to the academy in Sanborn. You could live at home and save money—"

"It's his decision, Helen! Let him alone. He'll go to whatever police academy he wants." Dad interrupts my mother but places his hand on hers to soften the rebuke.

I look across the breakfast table at them and smile. "I understand, Mom. Yeah, you're right, it would make sense to go to the academy nearby but this one's not that far away."

My brother snorts as he reaches for another piece of toast. "I'm sure the fact that Leah's going to be in Syracuse, an hour away, has nothing to do with your decision, right?" His voice lowers, and he gives me a jab in the arm. "I seriously don't know how you snagged her. Is she blind or something?"

Amy leans closer to him, snickering. "Jealous much, Seth?"

He knows she's kidding, but he blurts it out anyway. "Jealous? More like totally floored is all. Oh man—" He shakes his head looking at me. "She's sooo hot! And funny! And smart!" He leans in and jabs me with an elbow. "She gotta sister?"

"Nope. Just a brother."

His face falls. "Damn." It brightens again. "Cousins?"

Mom waves her hand at them to dismiss the bantering. "So you're going to check in at the academy after your visit with this... Margrit? I wish you'd stay here for a few more days. You've got a week until classes start."

It's hard to believe that they're actually going to miss me! A lot has happened since I've come back home. I look over at her. "Mom, I'll call you when I get there—both at Margrit's and then when I get to the school."

She sighs and then finishes the last of her coffee. She's worried. Even Seth hasn't left the nest yet, going to a college in Buffalo. She knows that this time when I leave, I'm not ever going to live with them again. But that's life. Birds leave the nest at some point, especially after a trial run that changed the course of my life.

Dad gets up and gives her a refill, shooting a smile at me. "I'm going to miss you at the store. These past few months have been profitable with you getting us set up with online ordering." He grins. "I still think you should have bought the Ford Fusion rather than that Japanese piece of junk, though."

This is his way of lightening the mood which is threatening to become maudlin—a joke between us. "That Japanese junk is more my style, Dad. I'll beat your car at the gas pumps, and I'm going to need that break, now that I'm back in school."

Amy fixes me with a grin. "So when can I visit you? Maybe I can go with you when you go to see Leah in Syracuse. That could be fun."

Seth's gaze flits to me and he smiles, continuing with his breakfast. Yeah, visit your girlfriend with a tagalong sister.

But it's Amy, and it *would* be fun. Leah and I are taking things slow. Having Amy there on a weekend visit would guarantee that. The funny thing is that raging hormones aside I want everything to be perfect for both of us before we make that step.

"Sure." I look over at my mother who now has a new

worry—Amy traveling by bus four hours away. "As long as Mom and Dad are cool with it, I am too."

I pick up my plate and take it to the dishwasher. When I turn, they all look at me. Dad with something I'd never thought I'd see in his eyes—pride in *me*! Mom just looks worried, as usual. Even Seth seems a little sad to see me going.

Amy gets up and comes over to put her arms around my waist. She's barely holding it together. I rub her hair and then kiss the top of her head. "I'll be back for Thanksgiving. And I'm not going to miss seeing you open my gift this Christmas. Promise."

My parents and Seth rise when they see me glance at the doorway. My bag is packed and waiting for me at the front door.

Seth's voice is light following my parents and I from the room. "So... you'll be a cop, soon. Does this mean no more traffic or speeding tickets for us?"

Dad answers, "He's not God, Seth. Besides which, you shouldn't be speeding."

I pause, and there's a lump in my throat when I give each of them a hug, ending with Amy. When I step out that door, I'm on my own—again. Except this time, I'm going with the family's blessing.

***

Three hours later, I pull into the town that's hauntingly familiar—Watertown. There's no way I'd be on my way to start a career in the police force if not for Mike. I park the car in front of the building where his office is. Even though it's Saturday, we had agreed to meet there. I suspect he's got an ulterior motive, though, something to do with one of his cases. No doubt he wants to get some input from his resident psychic on a missing person or dog.

I'm barely in the building when Chauncy comes lumbering out of Mike's office, his jowls loose with a long drool falling to the floor. He lets out a bark and then he's nosing my palm, looking for a pet or some kind of treat. He's looking more and more like Mike as time passes, even getting fatter.

"Chauncy!"

The voice that calls to him surprises me. Hilda? And then she rounds the corner, but her face glows when she spies me standing there. "Adam!"

I'm folded into her chest while her hands rub my back. "Hilda? What are you doing—"

"Adam!" Now Mike comes up to me, waiting to shake my hand while Hilda finishes the hug.

"Hey, Mike." My gaze flits over to Hilda when Mike's hand and mine shake. It comes to me in a flash, how he contacted her when he was looking for me, their subsequent phone calls, coffee dates and... I close my mind to anything more. I really don't want that detailed a picture of Mike's love life.

"So, they accepted you in the academy, kid?" Mike steps back and motions for us to follow him into his office.

I snicker at his back but shoot a look at Hilda to let her know I'm teasing. "Yeah. Figured if they'd take you, then I'd be a shoo-in."

"Just shows how low their standards are getting, I guess." But Mike's grinning, enjoying giving me the gears too.

"You two! Cut it out!" Hilda takes a spot next to Mike and pats his arm. Her head tilts to the side when she fixes her gaze on me. "I'm glad things worked out for you Adam, although I miss you at Rabbit Express."

Mike rolls his eyes. "Yeah, she's even got me doing a few deliveries to cover her dumbass nephew."

I don't have to ask about Philip. Mike's summed it up nicely. Once a dumbass, always a dumbass.

"So you two... you're an item now?" I know the answer, but I want to see Mike's response.

He puts his arm around Hilda's shoulder. "She even made me reach out to my daughter Amanda. Did you know I'm a granddaddy? I'm too young for that, but still, Molly's the cutest and smartest girl in the world! Not that I'm partial or anything."

Hilda looks up at him, and it's plain to see how crazy she is for the guy. "I'm not arguing the point. She's a doll! And have you noticed that Mike's lost weight?"

I hadn't, and I'm not sure he actually has but his cheeks aren't so fleshy, and they're not that ruddy color either. "Oh yeah?"

She laughs and gives him a poke in the ribs. "I think The Slip misses seeing Mike parked on a bar stool every night. He's discovered live theatre and long walks in the park are more fun."

He smiles down at her. "Because you drag me there."

Chauncy comes over nuzzling my hand again, "So no one ever came to claim this mutt?"

Mike's chest puffs out like a banty rooster. "Chauncy is no mutt, Adam! He may be homely as hell but he's got breeding! People actually call me for his stud services! I may be able to retire soon thanks to old Chaunce." He looks over at me and he's serious for once. "So, you and that girl still seeing one another?"

Hilda's eyes have lit up too, watching me closely. Who doesn't love a romance?

"I'm seeing Leah later today. Actually I'm spending a few days in Saranac to meet her family and friends, as well as catch up with Margrit. She'll be going to Syracuse U which isn't that far from where I'll be studying."

His eyebrows rise high. "Sounds serious."

"You have no idea, Mike." But it's not something I'm going to get into right then. Maybe down the road. "Let's have lunch. I want to show you my new car."

An hour later I'm back on the road, going down a highway that took me to the demon's destination. Little did it know that it would mean the end of its evil plan as well. Seeing the landscape transform becoming filled with mountains, their tops in a bluish haze in the distance is a far cry from the bus ride that horror-filled night.

I'll always carry the guilt and horror of what it did in Watertown to those women and Doug, but for now, I only want to leave it behind me.

Leah is before me.

A new life, where my psychic abilities are no longer something that I have to hide, nor something to show like a trick monkey's antics.

This is me. And I'm proud of who I am.

Finally.

The END

Author's Note…

Poor Adam. Every time he thought he had the world by the tail, he got bitten anyway! I enjoyed working with him, and was happy to see that it worked out…so far... for him.

I hope you enjoyed spending time with Adam, Leah, Margrit and Jake. They really grew on me in the writing of this book!

If this is your first exposure to my work, many of these characters thread through other works of mine, **'The Haunted Ones'**. Each of them is a stand alone novel, yes; there are no cliffhangers or continued tales. Having said that, it's nice to visit with them.

ABOUT MICHELLE DOREY

A multiple bestselling author, Michelle Dorey has written more than a dozen spine-chilling novels featuring ghosts, haunted houses and the supernatural.

A voracious reader of the masters like Stephen King and Dean Koontz, her debut novel was inspired by attending a Ghost Walk in the enigmatic city of Kingston, Ontario, Canada. Crawley House was inspired by a true tale of a family's nightmare, living in a Victorian era home.

"Expect the supernatural when the bedrock of a city is limestone. When this ancient rock is surrounded on three sides by water as my home town is... well, you have the perfect setting for eerie events--which of course is my cup of tea."

Wife and mother, Michelle is also a dog lover, human to Suki and Ruby. She loves them dearly, but for the last eight years on walks, they absolutely refuse to enter grounds of a beautiful historic cemetery near her home.

Michelle has written two complete series, The Hauntings Of Kingston and The Mystical Veil. She's currently at work on her latest, The Haunted Ones--set in upper New York State.

OTHER WORKS
BY
MICHELLE DOREY

THE HAUNTINGS OF KINGSTON SERIES

The city of Kingston is enigmatic; where the line between this world and the next becomes quite hazy. A ghostly series inspired by this historic and sometimes mysterious place. Each novel is a stand alone:

Crawley House
The Haunted Inn
The Ghosts Of Centre Street
The Haunting Of Larkspur Farm
The Ghosts Of Hanson House

THE MYSTICAL VEIL

Twenty four year old trust fund brat Keira Swanson finds out that her family has secrets. Secrets of the dead…

Legacy
Heritage
Forsaken
Ascendant

PARANORMAL SUSPENSE
The Haunted Ones

Ordinary people confront malevolent spirits in each of these eerie tales…

The Haunted Hideout
A Grave Conjuring
Haunted By The Succubus
The Haunted Gathering
The Haunted Reckoning
Graveyard Shift

SPECIAL BONUS:

The first two chapters of

The Haunted Gathering

Another Epidode of The Haunted Ones!

ABOUT THE HAUNTED GATHERING

On their annual girls' weekend three friends gather for a macabre reunion in this chilling tale of ghosts, hauntings and the occult.

Dara died almost a year ago, and her three closest surviving friends gather in accordance with her last wishes at Gabbinger's Reach—a once abandoned resort she planned on restoring to opulence.

The derelict property has been decaying for decades. Cindy the career woman thinks this is stupid. Melanie, the flighty one is fascinated. Becky, now a therapist is curious—why would Dara want them here?

They're enticed to stay by Dara's Last Will and Testament. Each of them are promised riches, all they need to do is remain here for two nights.

When darkness descends on the first evening, they laugh off the sudden appearance of small gifts. They're only a little startled by things crashing around in the kitchen. Someone's trying to spook them; big freaking deal—Cindy brought a gun!

Their bravado is tested when they begin to uncover long

held secrets. Secrets about each another, secrets about Dara, and long hidden secrets about the evil that infests the very walls of this place. Hungry evil relishing fresh victims.

At the same time their bonds of friendship are at the breaking point, the ravenous beast descends in a mighty fury. In a night of terror, they know they'll never be the same. If they survive.

Dara didn't.

The Haunted Gathering

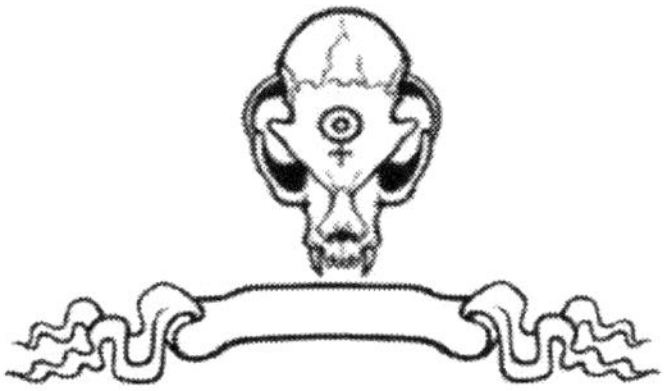

MICHELLE DOREY

The Haunted Ones 4

ONE

Rebecca finished typing the last entry into Bobbi Penstock's file. It had been a longer day than usual, cramming her schedule to clear up some time in September for the annual get-together. She clicked the mouse bringing up her personal email.

When Dara's email popped up, she smiled. *Finally* there'd be some details of where they'd meet. Trust Dara to leave everything to the last minute, just like in college. Some things never changed.

To: Becky, Melanie, Cindy

Date: Monday, June 28 at 10:43 PM

Subject: Our 7th Annual Reunion Bash

Hi ladies,

SEVEN years since Caltech! What the hell? Even crazier is the fact that I actually miss that place...sometimes.

I know you're on the edge of your seats waiting for details of our get-together (or as Melanie calls it "the gathering") At least I hope you are sitting down because...

I've got SUPER fantastic plans for our reunion this year.

I BOUGHT A FREAKING RESORT!

That's right. Dara Zuckerman is now the official owner of Gabbinger's Reach, in the Catskill Mountains.

And before you suggest I sign up for a few sessions of psycho-therapy with you, Becky, it was the deal of a lifetime. Too good to pass up! Rock-bottom sticker price.

I don't know how much you know about the Borsch belt in the Catskills, but in its heyday (1950s and 60s) it was THE place for rich New York Jewish folks to get away from the heat of the city to relax. I'm not going to go into the anti-Semitism that was rampant during that time in NYC, (which, thank God has changed), but the popularity of the area fell off during the 70s and 80s.

Like other resorts, Gabbinger's has been abandoned for DECADES! Sure, it needs work and MONEY, of which I've got tons. Thanks Daddy, for that at least. (sigh)

You're going to love it, Melanie, with the scenic mountains and the lake practically at our front door. Who knows with these buff construction guys, you may even finally get a boyfriend. Got to put yourself out there a bit, Mel. Put down the crystals, tarot cards and books and join the living instead of the dead. You might like it. (Teasing of course. You know I love you just the way you are.)

Don't worry about how rustic and primitive it is, Cindy. By SEPTEMBER, our accommodations will be TOTALLY revamped with every convenience you'd ever want.

(After what happened in Chicago, I owe you that much at least, although I know I was right doing it. All forgiven? If not, we can count on Becky to "therapy" us, just like back in the good old days sharing that house on campus. Remember the ice-cream incident? That could have gotten real ugly if not for Becky.)

Becky, give my regards to Hank. He's gonna have to cook for himself while you're gone but Boo Hoo. LOL

I know this is a far stretch from the glitzy Vegas trip, Cindy. Or traipsing over Mayan Ruins, Melanie...or even the seaside resort in Rockport, Becky... BUT it's my turn to choose the venue this year.

My turn, my resort. So there. Suck it up, Buttercups.

Besides which, I'm dying to show it to you, my oldest and dearest friends! Well...maybe not as it is today but what I'm going to DO with it!

Did I mention that the area is under consideration by the state for more casino expansion? That's where the REAL money is. Well that's one avenue that makes this worthwhile, but I've got some other ideas too. How about an Adults Only Spa? I don't care as long as they have full pockets for me to plunder. Hopefully you'll come up with more ideas!

I've had a crew up there for a month working. There's a section of the resort that's once more habitable for us. Don't worry, I'm going there tomorrow to crack the whip and make sure of it.

I'm attaching a few pics of the area as well as a map. Not sure the Google Car ever made it this far into the boonies.

Besties forever,

Dara

Rebecca sank back in the leather chair and exhaled slowly. Dara bought a resort in the Catskills? With the death of her father last year she now had total control of the estate, so why not? Still, maybe she was biting off more than she could chew. Delayed grief reaction? Trying hard to relive her father's dreams? But she had made a tidy profit when she'd sold that art gallery two years ago.

The intercom on her desk buzzed bringing her out of the reverie. "Yes?"

"Your eleven o'clock is here. Shall I send him in?" Gloria's low voice let her know that Jason Knox was probably perched on the edge of the chair in the waiting room. No doubt his knee was twitching, looking forward to unloading the slights and injustices he'd suffered at the hands of his domineering mother the past week. No matter that he was thirty-four and still living under his parents' roof with zero job prospects.

"Give me five, Gloria. I'm just finishing up an article." No need to tell her receptionist she was still pondering Dara's email.

What was that *Chicago* thing all about? Something happened there between Dara and Cindy? Maybe she'd give Cindy a call later to get the dirt. Probably Dara had done something thoughtless. Tact and diplomacy weren't her strong suits, whereas Cindy was people-smart. She had to be to make it in that cutthroat business.

Rebecca turned slightly to gaze out the window at the expanse of chrome and mirrored buildings. If she leaned closer there was even a partial view of the Olympic Mountains, maybe if it wasn't hazy and overcast. Prime office space in downtown Seattle. Not bad for a kid who grew up in neighboring Tacoma. Like Melanie and Cindy, she'd had to work two jobs in the summer to pay for tuition. Even so, she was still paying off her student loans.

Dara. How they'd ever hooked up with a trust-fund kid and became friends was still a wonder. But to give Dara credit, she *was* fun to hang with. There was never a dull moment with her antics. Maybe she'd finally found her place in life with this abandoned resort, breathing life into it.

She pushed the button on her desk signaling that she was ready for Jason Knox. She'd answer the email after his session.

Never knowing that by that time, Dara would be dead.

TWO

That September...

You didn't make her *funeral,* Cindy. This is the least that you can do!" Holding the phone in a death grip, Rebecca gritted her teeth so hard they clicked. It was bad enough that Cindy refused to tell her about the altercation she'd had with Dara in Chicago, but here she was trying to dodge the last request that Dara would ever make!

"Come on, Beck! Don't try to guilt me into going. As for the funeral, I was in *Australia*, for Pete's sake! Even if I decided to risk losing our biggest client and come back I still couldn't have made it in time." The exasperation in Cindy's voice bordered on being whiny.

"Look. All I'm saying is that it's the last thing we'll ever get to do for Dara. And what about Melanie? You know how close to Dara she is...or rather was. This will totally devastate her if we all don't show up at this Gabbinger's place. *She* needs our support if nothing else." Rebecca's eyes narrowed. Whatever had happened between Cindy and Dara had to be pretty rough if she was so willing to skip out on the dead woman's last request.

Cindy's tone softened, "Poor Mel. But it's just so morbid. I mean Dara drowned there. And that thing in her will is creepy as hell. Who makes a will before they're even thirty, anyway?"

"I know. I wondered about that too. Was she depressed? Why would she go swimming at night, *alone*?" It wasn't the first time that she wondered if Dara had been suicidal. But she hadn't talked to Dara in months. Not something she was proud of, but people have their own lives. They get busy.

"That was so *Dara*. Invincible. She paid the ultimate price for her recklessness." There was silence for a few beats, both of them picturing their friend. "Have you spoken to Melanie? I mean since the funeral."

"I texted her a few times, and when she didn't answer I finally called. She's adamant that we all go there, to honor Dara's wishes. She... Well, you'll see for yourself anyway, but...she's gotten even more obsessed with this spiritualism shit."

"Of course she has. She'll never change." Cindy's tone went from wistful to annoyed in the next breath. "That letter we all got from her lawyer...It wouldn't have killed him to give us more information to go on. Just be at Gabbinger's September twenty-first at four p.m. to honor Dara's last wishes. And we have to stay the weekend?"

Becky's voice hitched when she spoke. "Of course you know that Dara's birthday is September twenty-second . She would have been twenty-eight. Way too young to die."

"You think she left us anything in the will?"

"Cindy! Is that all you're—"

"NO!" Her voice became softer after Becky's chastisement. "Just wondering is all. None of us need it. Well...maybe Mel could use it. But money was never Melanie's thing, right? Give her a book about goblins and poltergeists, and she's lost in her own world."

"She's not as strong as the rest of us, Cindy. That sort of stuff is her crutch--escaping into make-believe. That way she doesn't have to risk real relationships. I don't think she's made any friends since us back in university. She needs us, Cindy. Say you'll come. It's only forty-eight hours. Surely you can put your career on hold for that long."

A long sigh followed, and Becky's head rose higher. When Cindy mumbled a soft, "I guess," her eyes closed with relief.

She decided to press ahead before Cindy had a chance to change her mind. "My flight arrives in Newark at one ten. Mel's getting there at noon. I've booked a car for us. You're welcome to drive with us."

"How far is it from the airport?" Cindy's voice drooped with resignation.

"Two hours. Seriously, we might even manage to have fun, you know. I'm bringing wine. We can count on Mel for weed. We'll celebrate Dara's birthday as if she were there." Becky tried to sound upbeat, barely pulling it off. Yes. Cindy was right. This was downright weirdly morbid.

Still, it would be good to see Mel and Cindy. But the reunion bash with just the three of them, where Dara had actually died, was going to be sad.

To say the least. Partying at the spot where one of your best friends died? She shuddered inwardly.

"Fine. I'll book the flight and see you tomorrow. This place better have a damn bathroom! I'm not using some outhouse or something. And that lawyer, Anthony Wilson, better have it well stocked with food and drink."

"Thanks, Cindy. I also want to know what went down with you and Dara in Chicago."

"Don't push your luck, Becky." This was followed by a click.